CHEERLEADERS

#38

TALKING BACK

LISA NORBY

SCHOLASTIC INC.
New York Toronto London Auckland Sydney

ISBN 0-590-41370-8

12 11 10 9 8 7 6 5 4 3 2 1   8 9/8 0 1 2 3/9

Printed in the U.S.A.   01

First Scholastic printing, February 1988

TALKING BACK

CHEERLEADERS

CHAPTER

"This is definitely the most ridiculous assignment I ever had," David Duffy told the cheerleaders. "Interviewing a psychic! Can you imagine? No one really believes in that stuff. And I'm sure no one in Tarenton is even interested in reading about Madame Magda Halevy."

The cheerleaders exchanged nervous glances. Maybe it was true that none of them believed in psychic powers. But they were all curious about Tarenton's newest celebrity. Why else had they gathered around Duffy as soon as practice ended to pump him for information?

"Isn't it true that Madame Magda helped the police find that lost child up in Franklin County?" Jessica Bennett asked Duffy. "I saw that on the TV news."

"That's right," Sean Dubrow put in.

Speaking into an imaginary microphone, he

dropped his voice an octave until it sounded remarkably like the gruff, gravelly baritone of one of the popular local news anchormen. "We're here at the Stag Mountain hunting cabin, where just minutes ago, little Jamie McFarland was found safe and sound, just as our Madame Magda Halevy predicted on last night's show."

"I remember that!" Tara Armstrong gasped. "Madame Magda predicted Jamie would be found in a hunter's cabin. And he was!"

Duffy looked mildly disgusted. "Come on, guys," he pleaded. "Give me a break. We all know that Madame Magda was just guessing, like anyone else. You don't really think that she has some sort of special powers!"

Tara gave her coppery hair a defiant shake. "Well, she was right, wasn't she? How could she know that?"

"Because," said Duffy, "there is nothing *on* Stag Mountain except trees and hunters' cabins. There must be at least fifty cabins up there, and a lot of times the owners don't even bother to lock them, the area is so remote. And the cabins don't have anything valuable in them anyway. It's sort of a tradition that if strangers get caught in a storm or whatever, they're welcome to spend the night. Anyway, it stands to reason that when the lost kid found a cabin he'd go inside looking for food and a place to sleep."

"But there was more to the story than that," Peter Rayman reminded him. "She said little Jamie would be found sound asleep on a plaid bedspread."

2

Tara's eyes opened wide with amazement. "And he was?"

Peter shrugged. "Ask the expert."

Tara spun in Duffy's direction. "Well?" she demanded.

"Well, yes . . ." Duffy admitted.

Jessica and Hope Chang exchanged knowing smiles and simultaneously broke into the opening bars of the *Twilight Zone* theme: "Da-da-da-da . . . da-da-da-da," they chanted.

Everyone except Duffy and Tara broke up laughing.

"It *is* something to think about," Peter said when he had regained his composure. "Maybe there's something to this ESP stuff after all. I mean, this lady *knew*, right? I heard her say on TV that she had a mental picture of the room where the little boy was found."

"Be serious, Rayman!" Duffy shot back. "You aren't dumb enough to believe that. Haven't you ever heard of coincidence? Besides, a plaid bedspread isn't exactly unusual decor for a hunting cabin, is it?"

"Good point," Hope agreed.

Olivia Evans took a deep breath and tried very hard to stay calm. Even though she and Duffy weren't as deeply involved as they once were, he was still her special friend. And it bothered her to see him getting into an argument with the squad.

Duffy is a great guy, Olivia thought. He always has something bright and clever to add to the group. But he expects people to agree with

3

his opinions, and when they don't, sometimes he doesn't accept that very well.

Was Duffy getting worse now that he had his once-a-week teen radio show on WGCV? Sometimes Olivia thought so, but she couldn't be sure. Maybe she was just more critical lately. There had been a time when everything Duffy said or did seemed perfect to her. Maybe it was natural that she was getting over that stage.

At any rate, she was determined to stay out of this discussion. She didn't care one bit about this Magda Halevy woman. For that matter, she had never understood why people were so interested in things like ESP and UFOs and astrology. Wasn't reality complicated enough?

Olivia just wanted the conversation to end so that Duffy would take her home, but that didn't seem about to happen. Undeterred by his clash with Peter, Duffy was launching into a description of his interview with Madame Magda.

"You wanted to know what I found out, so I'll tell you," he said to the group. "For one thing, there's this business of calling herself *Madame*. How fakey can you get? And her accent! Supposedly, the woman is Hungarian, but I did some research and I found out that before she turned up here she was living in Detroit."

Duffy grinned triumphantly. "Detroit!" he repeated, as if that were the final proof of his argument.

"What's wrong with Detroit?" Hope asked.

Hope looked so petite and adorable in her pink angora sweater and softly flared gray skirt that it seemed almost impossible that she could ever get angry with anyone. But Olivia recognized the slight tightening in Hope's voice, and she knew that Duffy must have a lecture coming to him.

"I'll have you know I have relatives in Detroit," Hope told Duffy. "And they're Chinese. Chinese Americans. So I don't see what's so ridiculous about Madame Magda coming from there. And I don't see why that proves she isn't Hungarian."

"She got you on that one," Peter put in.

Duffy looked ready to give in, but Hope wasn't finished with him yet.

"You think you're being so rational. But really you're not. You're thinking in stereotypes. Where this person is from has nothing to do with whether or not her powers are genuine."

"What I don't understand," said Jessica, changing the subject, "is why someone would pretend to be a psychic if it wasn't true. I heard she doesn't charge for her consultations."

"True," said Duffy. "But maybe she just likes feeling important."

That's a motive you should understand, Olivia wanted to say. But she bit her tongue and kept quiet.

"Don't you know that a lot of these feats psychics perform are really just magic tricks?" Duffy went on, looking straight at Tara. "I just hate to see people like you being taken in."

Tara bristled. "What do you mean, people like me?"

5

"Well you know . . . uh . . . people who, uh . . ." Duffy hemmed and hawed.

"He means gullible people," said Sean helpfully. "Easy marks. And I, for one, agree. Sensible people don't pay any attention to this kind of stuff. At least, not guys. Why do you think they put the astrology column on the women's page of the *Lighter*?"

This conversation is really getting out of hand, Olivia told herself. In a minute, it wasn't going to be just Hope versus Duffy, or Duffy versus Tara, but an all-out war of the sexes.

Olivia decided to resort to humor to derail the argument before it could get started. "Well, I just wish I had a psychic to tell me what we should do for a routine at the exhibition game next week," she said brightly. "Does anyone have a suggestion?"

Sean shot Olivia a look of gratitude. He had realized belatedly that none of the girls considered his comment funny, and he was happy that he wasn't going to have to defend it.

Unfortunately, Duffy was too wrapped up in his own train of thought to know when he was being rescued. "That, Olivia, is exactly the attitude people like Madame Magda count on. People don't want to solve their own problems anymore. So they look for an easy way out. They go to a fortune-teller. Or a psychic. But don't you see, you're just playing right into their hands."

"Don't I see!" Olivia was incensed. "I see that you're acting like a stuffy professor, David

6

Duffy. So don't talk down to me. You have no right."

Olivia picked up her backpack and her coat and headed out the door without another word. She had already missed the school bus, so she would have to walk half a mile to the nearest public bus stop. But she didn't care. She felt like taking a walk in the fresh air. And it would certainly be better than having to put up with Duffy when he was in one of his know-it-all moods.

Duffy looked completely surprised that Olivia had walked out on him. "What brought that on?" he asked. "What did I say?"

Hope glared at Sean. "Don't you dare say, 'just like a woman,'" she threatened.

Sean raised his hands in a gesture of surrender. "I'm not saying anything," he promised. "I wouldn't even think of it."

They all walked out the front door of the school together, just in time to see Patrick Henley's van turn into the parking lot and draw even with Olivia. Patrick must have offered Olivia a lift, because they could see her shake her head and point in the direction of the bus stop.

Patrick drove over to where the squad was gathered and pulled to a stop. "Is anything wrong?" he asked.

"Just the usual," said Duffy. "I'm sure it was all my fault. I just haven't figured out why yet, so I'd better go after Livvy and get her to explain it to me."

Duffy strode off and Tara hopped into the van.

"Anyone else need a ride?" Patrick asked.

"No thanks," said Hope. "Sean is taking me home. It's right on his way."

"Same here," said Peter.

Melissa Brezneski, the cheerleading alternate, had left practice early.

That left Jessica. Patrick gave her a questioning look.

"I'm taking the bus," Jessica said quickly. "I like to. No kidding. Walking to the bus stop gives me a chance to collect my thoughts after practice."

"I don't think it will be so calming today," Patrick commented. "You'll just run into Duffy and Olivia and have to hear the end of their argument. So hop in."

Jessica hesitated.

"Oh, come on," Tara urged.

Jessica accepted the invitation reluctantly and got into the van next to Tara. Soon, she and Patrick were engaged in a lively conversation about Patrick's moving business and his new partner, Tony Pell.

"Tony is cleaning out the back room," Patrick told her. "You know, the one we were always going to fix up as an office. Well, he's finally doing it. He moved the rolltop desk back there yesterday."

"That desk!" sighed Jessica. "Remember how we found it at the dump? It was in beautiful condition, but when we got it back to the garage, it turned out that one leg was shorter than the others."

Patrick laughed. "I remember. Wasn't that strange? We tried cutting a little bit off the longer legs, but somehow they never came out quite even. I was sure that by the time we got them all the same, it would be a desk for midgets."

We . . . we . . . we . . . we . . .

Tara wanted to scream. She knew she was being childish. Just because Jessica and Patrick had broken up, and Tara had started seeing Patrick, there was no reason why he and Jessica couldn't talk about old times. Still, all this "we did this, we did that" talk hurt her deeply.

Patrick had never mentioned to her that he had a plan to fix up the back room. He'd never told her the story about the desk, either.

Was it possible that Patrick had been a different kind of person when he was with Jessica? The two of them seemed to have such an easy relationship. And they certainly had no trouble finding things to talk about.

Tara didn't always find talking to Patrick all that easy. He had such a strong physical presence — wide shoulders, muscular arms, penetrating blue eyes, and that distinctive, slightly crooked smile. And he had the confident, outgoing personality that went with his looks. Tara liked to think that the two of them were alike, at least in that way. They were both extroverts.

But when Patrick was with Jessica, he showed another side of his personality — a sort of playfulness that rarely emerged when he and Tara were together.

Sitting there, stuck in between them as they rattled on about "old times" — really not that long ago — Tara felt almost as if they were the couple and she were the interloper.

She started to fantasize about what would happen if the van pulled up in front of her house right now. What if she just got out and said, "Thanks for the ride." Would Patrick and Jessica forget that they were no longer a couple and drive off together?

Maybe her romance with Patrick would turn out like that season of *Dallas*, where a whole year's worth of episodes turned out to be a dream. Maybe she was dreaming *right now*.

Not a chance, Tara scolded herself. She mustn't let her imagination run away with her. There was no way she was going to lose Patrick.

"Tara! Are you all right?"

The question jolted her back to her senses. From the worried looks on Patrick's and Jessica's faces they must have been trying to get her attention for some time.

"Oh, sure," she said. "You know me. I was just daydreaming."

"You looked as if you were in a trance," Jessica joked. "Better not let David Duffy see you like that. He'll think you're trying to be the next Madame Magda."

"Who?" asked Patrick.

Tara started to explain, but before she could finish a complete sentence, she realized that Patrick was looking at Jessica to answer the question. And sure enough, she quickly told the whole story, complete with her impression of Sean doing his impression of the TV anchorman.

Patrick seemed to be thoroughly enjoying the story. "Of course, I agree with Duffy," he said. "That psychic stuff is all a put-on."

"Right." Jessica nodded. "We were just teasing Duffy. Sometimes he takes himself too seriously."

"Wait a second," Tara objected. "I wasn't kidding. I believe in psychic phenomena. At least, there might be something to it."

Patrick and Jessica stared at her. Now she really felt like the third wheel — flighty, irrational Tara, showing off in front of two rational adults. "I just wouldn't rule it out," she said, retreating. "I mean, why not keep an open mind?"

"Sure," Jessica said, a shade condescendingly. "Why not?"

They stopped in front of the Bennett house, and Jessica got out of the van. Tara watched her stride gracefully up the walk towards her front door. Patrick seemed completely relaxed. Obviously, the two of them saw no problem in being just friends.

Tara, on the other hand, felt as if she'd just been through a minor ordeal. Her stomach felt funny. Her palms were damp. This wasn't like her at all. She had always felt sorry for people who were jealous. It was such a waste of time!

Tara was determined that she wasn't going to let herself get caught in that trap. She was going to find some way to deal with the problem, and soon.

CHAPTER

2

"Let's do a few pliés now, and remember, keep your feet in the proper position."

Olivia watched Marian Van Heusen demonstrate a plié. The dance teacher had an elegantly arched neck, a long-waisted body, and strong, supple feet. She wore a dark brown leotard that almost matched the color of her skin, and her hair was pulled back and held in place by a white chiffon scarf. Every move she made was elegant and assured.

Then Olivia looked down at her own feet, splayed outward in a parody of the position Marian was demonstrating.

"This looks good when other people do it," she whispered to Melissa, who was standing at the barre next to her. "So why is it that I feel like a duck?"

Melissa giggled. "Don't worry," she said. "This

is just the first part of the class. It's good for your posture. Later, we do a combination of dance and aerobics."

Melissa attended the aerobics class at Marian's studio every afternoon when there was no cheerleading practice. Today, she was feeling especially eager to get going since she had missed yesterday's practice for a dentist appointment.

Olivia, on the other hand, wasn't at all sure she was going to enjoy herself. She had accepted Melissa's invitation because it seemed like a good way to get to know her better. Now, somewhat doubtfully, she looked over the class. It was a mixed group — a few young married people, several athletes from the Deep River football team who were trying to keep in shape during the off-season, and one gray-haired lady who must have been over seventy but who was in wonderful shape. Except for Melissa, and of course the teacher, Marian, none of the class were real dancers, and they all looked as clunky as Olivia felt.

Olivia knew, in an off-handed way, that a lot of people considered her pretty. She had feathery brown hair and deep dimples when she smiled and a small, wiry gymnast's body. Most of the time, Olivia was fairly well satisfied with the way she looked. Watching Marian, though, she wished she were a different type altogether. It must be wonderful to be elegant . . . sophisticated-looking . . . glamorous.

Marian was also creative, another quality Olivia envied. According to Melissa, the exercise instructor had developed her own program. She was a choreographer, too, and she even composed and arranged her own music for the tapes she used in class.

If she can do all that, Olivia wondered, why can't I come up with just one idea for a routine that we can work up in time for the exhibition game with Danville?

After a few minutes, as Melissa had promised, the pace of the class picked up. The exuberant, challenging routine shook Olivia out of her self-critical mood. The whole class was having fun now, especially Olivia and Melissa, who were limber enough from cheerleading to do all the exercises with panache.

"I'm getting better, better, better . . ." sang the voice on Marian's music tape. "I'm getting better every day. . . ."

That's right, thought Olivia, exhilarated by the pounding beat of the music. So what if I'm not glamorous. So what if I'm not creative. At least I know I'm getting better at the things I care about doing.

By the time the class ended, she was feeling positive about herself again. Apparently, so was the rest of the group. When the last chords of the song died out, everyone clapped, cheering their own efforts. "I haven't had so much fun since I used to do the jitterbug," the lady in her seventies said happily.

Olivia and Melissa changed into their street clothes and left the studio, stopping for a cold drink at the juice bar next door. "I'm really glad you could come to class today," Melissa said. "Even though I enjoy Marian's routines, I don't know anyone in the class. It's much easier to keep going to class when you have someone to go with. A little bit of moral support goes a long way."

"It sure does," Olivia agreed.

Automatically, she thought of Duffy. Yesterday, she had very much wanted someone who would help her think of ideas for a new routine. But Duffy had been no help at all. First, he had gotten the entire squad riled up with his lecture on gullibility. Then he had insulted her when she was only trying to rescue him from making himself look stupid.

Later, Duffy had picked her up at the bus stop and they made up the quarrel. But by then, there had been no time to discuss cheerleading routines. Maybe it was her imagination, but lately it seemed that Duffy's concerns were always important enough to talk about. Hers seldom were.

"Do you think Duffy is getting worse?" she asked Melissa abruptly.

Melissa looked bewildered. "Worse than what?"

Olivia laughed. "I don't know. It just seems to me that he doesn't give me much moral support. He gets so wrapped up in his own bright ideas."

"It seems to me that he's always been like that," Melissa said. "He just loves to talk, you know that. But so what? I think Duffy is really attractive. You're lucky that he's so crazy about you."

Melissa took a sip of her pineapple juice. "Come to think of it," she added, "you have two great guys crazy about you. Most girls I know would be happy to be going out with either one of them. You must be having a great time."

Olivia sighed. "Sometimes," she admitted. "Other times, I just feel confused."

Last year, when she was the only junior on the cheerleading squad, Olivia had indeed felt lucky to be going out with Walt Manners. But she had felt hurt and rejected when Walt cut off their relationship sooner than necessary to leave Tarenton for a summer job as an apprentice at a summer-stock theater. Then he went on to New York to study at Columbia University. And she had met Duffy, and once again she felt that she had found the ideal guy for her.

Now Walt was back in town, taking a semester off from Columbia to earn some money and rethink his priorities. And so far, his arrival in town had caused Olivia nothing but turmoil.

In many ways, Walt and Duffy were opposites. Walt Manners was friendly and sincere, but his stocky body and round face could hardly be considered handsome. Duffy had angular good looks and was a sharp dresser; his glib sense of humor and quick mind made him interesting to be with. But Duffy's charm also made him harder to get to know. Even though Walt had been away for months, Olivia still found him easier to talk to.

Logic told her that she should avoid getting

too involved with either boy. But why shouldn't she date both of them? Other girls dated more than one guy at a time, didn't they? Or at least, she could see Duffy and still be friends with Walt.

"Maybe I should enjoy having two guys competing for me," Olivia told Melissa. "But most of the time, I just feel guilty. Right now, for example, I'd love to call up Walt and talk to him about the routine for the Danville game. He loves thinking up new ideas. Look at the great idea he came up with for the stunt we did with scooters."

"So why not call him?" Melissa asked.

"Because if I do, I'll feel that I'm being disloyal to Duffy," Olivia explained.

Melissa arched an eyebrow skeptically. "I think you're taking this too seriously," she said. "You're not that committed to either of them. Besides, I notice that Duffy's feelings for you don't stop him from criticizing the cheerleaders in his column for the *Lighter*. For that matter, you told me Walt didn't let your relationship stop him from taking that out-of-town job last summer."

"Maybe you're right," Olivia agreed, as she counted out the money to pay for her juice. "Still, I can't help feeling that this is different, even if I'm not sure why."

But later that evening, as she struggled to finish her English lit homework, Olivia found herself thinking over what Melissa had said. It was true that Duffy always put his career first.

He hadn't even bothered to ask her advice before accepting the offer to do his weekly teen radio show!

And Walt was no better. He seemed to think that he could waltz in and out of Tarenton, and in and out of her life, whenever it suited him.

So why am I the one feeling guilty? Olivia asked herself.

Melissa was right, she decided. From now on, she was not going to let Duffy and Walt make her miserable. Let *them* worry about which one she would choose.

Olivia closed her book and went over to the full-length mirror that was attached to the back of her closet door. She practiced striking a femme fatale pose. Maybe I'm not the glamorous, sultry type by nature, she told herself, but that's all the more reason why I should enjoy this situation while it lasts.

The thing that bothered her most about her face were her eyebrows. Thick, dark, and straight, they were her most noticeable feature. More times than she could remember, Olivia had been told that they were distinctive. They drew attention to her eyes, people said. They were chic, others told her. They gave her face individuality. Look at Brooke Shields.

Olivia, however, had never been convinced. She thought her eyebrows made her look like a little kid.

So why not do something about it! Feeling rebellious, she grabbed a pair of tweezers from her dresser. At first, she was just going to thin her brows a little bit. But she felt so daring, that she decided to keep on. She plucked a hair here, another there, then a few more, and so on until her eyebrows had been reduced to a pair of pencil-thin arcs.

Next, she rummaged through the makeup tray in the top drawer of her dresser and found a seldom-used eyeliner pencil, a compact containing eye shadow in three shades of violet, and another containing shades of blusher. Her first experiments weren't too successful, but after several tries she found a way to highlight her cheekbones and emphasize the shape of her full lower lip. Even more amazing, her heavily made-up eyes transformed her face.

The cute, athletic, but slightly dull Olivia Evans had disappeared. Instead, the mirror revealed a new Olivia — one with deep-set, brooding eyes, dramatic coloring, and an enigmatic expression.

"Mom will have a fit when she sees my new look," Olivia muttered to herself. "But she'll just have to get used to the new me. And so will Duffy and Walt!"

CHAPTER

Tara Armstrong parked her Chevy on the corner of Hamilton Avenue and fished around inside her oversized hobo bag until she found her address book. Checking carefully, she convinced herself that the address she had gotten from telephone information matched the one on the door of the red brick house just across the street.

What a disappointment!

Ever since yesterday afternoon, when Duffy told the squad about his interview with Madame Magda, Tara had been dying to meet her. She didn't exactly believe in psychic phenomena. At least that was what she kept telling herself. But the subject fascinated her.

In school today, she had been able to think about nothing else. And luckily, since there was no practice, she had been able to get Madame

Magda's address and track it down in the Chevy. Now, she wasn't sure what to do next.

Hamilton Avenue ran through Tarenton's oldest neighborhood, an area of quiet streets and sprawling Victorian houses. In her imagination, Tara had pictured Madame Magda living in one of those romantic old homes. A house like that could easily have a ghost or two in the attic, Tara thought, or even an evil spirit lurking in the basement.

Instead, 847 Hamilton was the most ordinary house possible — a one-story brick contemporary, with a picture window and an attached garrage. Of course, Madame Magda had just arrived in town and was probably renting the house. Still, it was difficult to imagine that anyone who possessed special powers could live in such an ordinary setting.

Tara was tempted to start the car and drive away. Then she changed her mind. As long as I came this far, she told herself, I might as well at least have a look at the famous Madame Magda.

Boldly, Tara marched up to the front porch of 847 and rang the bell. On the first ring, the door swung open.

"Yess, and vot can I do to hailp you," said a thickly accented voice.

Tara found herself face to face with a slender, brown-haired woman wearing a black dress and half a dozen silver bracelets on each arm. The dress was a bit sophisticated by Tarenton standards, at least for the middle of the day, but nothing that out of the ordinary.

Tara was starting to feel silly. She realized that she had been expecting floor-length robes and a turban. Or maybe a wizened old lady with a crocheted shawl over her shoulders.

Worse yet, she hadn't given any thought to what she would ask when she actually met Madame Magda. She had just barged right up to her door with no plan at all. Now here she was, feeling like a complete idiot.

"I'm sorry," she apologized. "I was looking for Madame Magda Halevy. I must have the wrong house."

"Nonsense, my dear. Zeese is ze place you were searching for. I am Madame Magda. Come right in."

Before Tara could flee, Madame Magda took her by the elbow and guided her into the living room. Tara looked around nervously. There wasn't a crystal ball in sight, just a television and a few books stacked neatly on the coffee table.

"Sit down. Sit down," Madame Magda urged. "Don't be nervous."

Tara noticed that when Madame Magda became impatient, her accent evaporated. Duffy was right, she told herself, this woman is a complete fraud.

"I see you have trouble in love," Madame Magda said, as if this were the most obvious thing in the world.

Tara was caught off guard. "You do? How do you know that?"

Madame Magda tilted her head to one side and smiled knowingly. "I feel zeese tings," she said. "And I see zeese in your aura. Is very troubled."

"My aura!" Tara glanced around, as if expecting to see some waves emanating from her head. "Do I have an aura? What's it look like?"

But Madame Magda didn't seem to hear. She sank into an easy chair across from the couch where Tara was sitting and leaned back, her eyes half closed.

"Ah yes," she said breathlessly. "I see your man now. Someone you have been close to."

Then she frowned. "But wait. Zeese is not good news. Not good. He eeze with someone else."

"He eeze! I mean, he is?" Tara felt her heart racing. "Who?"

"I see no face." Madame shook her head. "No face at all. But I see a uniform. A red and white uniform. What kind, I don't know."

Tara's face flushed with anger. "That's all right," she said. "I know exactly what kind of uniform it is."

Madame Magda sat up and opened her eyes wide. She looked as if she had just awakened from deep sleep. "I'm sorry," she said groggily, her accent gone. "These pictures come to me. I can't control them. But I don't like to tell people unhappy things. I hope you are not too sad."

"Don't worry," Tara assured her. "I'm not sad. I'm angry. My boyfriend is two-timing me, and I'm not going to let him get away with it."

Tara thanked Madame Magda for her help

and hurried back to the car. She was sure she knew what Madame Magda's vision meant. Another girl was moving in on Patrick. And judging by the red and white uniform that Madame Magda had "seen," that girl could only be Jessica Bennett. No doubt Jessica was probably sorry that she and Patrick had broken up, and now she was trying to steal him back.

For the next half hour, Tara drove around town, looking for Patrick's van in the parking lots of the hangouts where he usually stopped for an after-work snack.

At least, she thought ruefully, I'm dressed for a confrontation. She was wearing her new leather jacket, a gift from her father. The leather was dyed a warm, carmelly shade, halfway between gold and tan, and it was so soft it felt like butter to the touch. Patrick hadn't seen the jacket yet, and she'd been looking forward to showing it to him. She'd chosen the rest of her outfit, her bone-colored corduroy slacks and white cowl-neck sweater, because she knew they'd look great with it.

All day long she'd been thinking of how Patrick would react when he saw her for the first time in that jacket. He'd be bowled over!

Now she almost wished she could bowl him over, literally. She was sure Madame Magda's vision meant that Patrick and Jessica were together this afternoon.

On her second trip past the Pancake House on Main Street, she spotted Patrick's van, the one with the H & T logo painted on the back doors.

Trying to control her temper, she eased the Chevy into the adjacent parking space and strode inside.

There was no sign of Patrick anywhere. And no Jessica.

But she did see Nancy Goldstein and Nick Stewart sitting together in one of the front booths. Blond, blue-eyed Nick was Tarenton High's handsomest, and youngest, teacher. Tara had once had quite a crush on him. But that was before she found out that he was a teacher, and before he realized that she was still a high school student.

Tara still thought Nick was one of the dreamiest men she had ever seen. But since he was beyond her reach, she was happy that he was dating Nancy Goldstein, who was home on a visit from Brown University because her father was ill. Nancy's dark hair and eyes made a good contrast to Nick's blondness. They were a cute couple. And since Nancy was a former cheerleader, Tara felt a kind of proprietary pride in the fact that she was the one who'd introduced them to each other. At least Nick was going out with one of her group.

Today, though, she had no time to think about Nick and Nancy's relationship. She strode over to their booth, hands on her hips, and demanded, "Have you seen Patrick?"

Nancy frowned. It wasn't polite of Tara to just come over and start interrogating her about Patrick without a word of greeting.

Nick finally answered the question. "Patrick was with us," he said, "but I think he went across the street to the newsstand."

"What about Jessica Bennett?" Tara pressed on. "Where did she go?"

Nick looked startled. "Jessica? What makes you think she was here?"

"I know she was." Tara laughed bitterly. "Let's call it a vision."

"Then your vision was wrong," Nancy informed her.

"It wasn't my vision," Tara said. "It was that psychic's, Madame Magda. She *saw* Patrick and Jessica together. I'm sure of it."

Nick and Nancy exchanged looks. Obviously, they thought Tara was out of her mind.

"Maybe she's here and we just don't know it," Nick joked. "Maybe she's invisible." He pretended to signal for the waitress. "I guess we'd better order her some food. Oh waitress! How about a Belgian waffle for our friend. She could use the calories, since she's so thin we can't even find her."

"Okay, okay. So I was wrong." Tara sank down on the seat next to Nancy. She didn't know what to think about Jessica and Patrick, but she couldn't stand to have Nick and Nancy treating her like a crazy kid. It was too humiliating!

Maybe Madame Magda had been wrong. Tara tried to put the subject out of her mind and answer Nancy's questions about cheerleading.

After a minute or so, Tara looked at the bundle on the seat between them. Wrapped in a transparent plastic dry cleaner's bag was a pleated skirt and a sweater. Both in the familiar red and white colors of Tarenton High.

"What's that?" Tara choked out, moving away from the plastic bag as if she'd seen a poisonous snake inside it.

"My old cheerleading uniform," Nancy said. "What does it look like? There's a costume party coming up at my sorority later this year. So I thought I'd get my old uniform cleaned and take it back to school with me. I just picked it up an hour ago."

Suddenly, it was all clear. Nancy and Nick must have been at the dry cleaner's at the very moment Madame Magda had her vision. *That* was what the psychic had seen! A guy she still cared for and his new love — *and* a Tarenton High cheerleading outfit. After all, Madame Magda had never said that the girl in her vision was actually wearing the cheerleader's uniform.

Tara felt a flood of conflicting emotions. Relief that her suspicions about Patrick and Jessica were wrong. And excitement at realizing that Madame's vision had been proven true.

"This is amazing," she said. "Don't you see? That's exactly what Madame Magda told me. And how could she know? I never mentioned that I was a cheerleader. She hasn't even been in town long enough to know that we wear red and white uniforms. She's so right, it's creepy."

"Wait a second," protested Nick. "I thought you said this Madame Magda person saw Patrick and Jessica. Now you're saying she saw me and Nancy. And at the dry cleaners?"

"Right," insisted Tara.

"I don't get it," said Nancy. "What's the point of having visions about that?" She giggled. "I mean, if you wanted to know, I would have told you."

Tara didn't want to get into a discussion about how she'd once cared about Nick, long before she'd fallen in love with Patrick. "I can't exactly explain it," she told them. "But believe me, everything that woman told me was true. It's uncanny. She really does have second sight."

Tara hurried out of the Pancake House and headed for her car. Patrick was standing there waiting for her, grinning with that sexy, crooked smile of his. "You look great," he said. "Is that a new jacket?"

She had forgotten all about the jacket, and now it didn't seem important anymore. She ran up to Patrick and flung her arms around him, giving him a big kiss.

"Better be careful," he warned, "These are my work clothes. I wouldn't want you to get your new outfit smudged."

"Who cares about a little smudge?" Tara exulted. "I'm just glad to have you back again."

"Back? Where have I been?" For a fleeting instant Patrick looked at Tara as if she were crazy. But she just kissed him again, and he decided to forget about logic for the time being.

Tara was one great-looking girl, and she was always so full of warmth and enthusiasm. So what if she acted a little flakey at times, Patrick asked himself. What harm was there in that?

CHAPTER

Olivia could hardly wait to try out her new image. She had shortened one of her skirts to near mini-length, and she was wearing it with an oversized striped jersey topped by one of Duffy's cast-off shirts and two belts, loosely buckled so that they hung around her hips. But it was her new makeup that made all the difference. She could hardly wait to see her friends' reactions.

She was in no hurry, though, to find out how her mother would react. To avoid a confrontation, she ate breakfast early, then stayed in her room, working on her hair, until it was time to leave for school. When she heard the bus come down the street, she grabbed her bag and sprinted for the door. "Gotta run now, Mom," she said cheerily, as she breezed past her mother.

Briefly, she caught sight of her mother's expression, a sort of dazed astonishment. She knew her mother disapproved of heavy makeup, so there would definitely be a long discussion at dinner. But that wasn't her fault! Mom disapproved of any kind of new development in her life, almost on principle.

The kids who caught the bus at her stop were mostly younger, and Olivia sat by herself for the ride to school. The first person she met in the front hall was Sean Dubrow, sauntering by on his way to his locker. "Hey there, Olivia," he said conversationally as their paths crossed. "What's up? Observing National Eye Shadow Week?"

"If I am, that's better than honoring National Stupidity Month," she shot back.

That lame retort didn't bother Sean in the slightest. He just grinned serenely and went on his way.

Olivia watched him go, trembling with hurt and anger. It was just Sean's way to come up with a smart remark. Half the time, his flip comments didn't mean a thing. But of course, he had brought her down to earth with a thud. Did she really look ridiculous? Was it possible that all the kids she passed in the halls were turning away to snicker and exchange remarks as soon as she was out of earshot?

Nervously, Olivia ducked into the girls' bathroom to check her appearance in the mirror. But as luck would have it, that territory was already occupied by Diana Tucker and Holly Hudson, who were in the middle of one of their arguments. Diana was not Olivia's favorite person. Ever since she transferred to Tarenton High, she had been scheming to cause trouble for the cheerleaders so that she could worm her way into a place on the squad. Diana had failed to get herself chosen as squad alternate — luckily Melissa had bested her in the tryouts — but her friendship with Holly, who was president of the Pompon Squad, gave Diana plenty of opportunities to cause trouble.

When she saw Olivia, Diana gave her blonde hair one final flip with the brush and stalked out of the room, though not before making it obvious that she had taken in all the details of Olivia's appearance. Holly, who was a good kid in spite of her friendship with Diana, moved over to make room in front of the mirror. "You look nice," Holly told Olivia sincerely. "Did you change your hair? I can't figure out what's different about you."

Olivia wanted to laugh at that one. No one in school wore more makeup than Holly. But it did reassure her to realize that compared to Holly, who looked like a raccoon wearing earrings, her own image was still fairly conservative.

On the whole, the strangest thing about the rest of the day was that most people didn't seem to react to her new image one way or another. And after practice that afternoon, when she cornered the other girls in the locker room and asked for their opinions, they were divided:

Jessica Bennett had hemmed and hawed, then admitted that she thought Olivia had looked better with a more natural look.

Melissa agreed with Jessica, much to Olivia's disappointment.

Hope, on the other hand, voted in favor of the new look. "I think you look much more sophisticated," she said, after studying Olivia's face intently, as if it were a new music score or a set of Latin vocabulary words. "I wouldn't change my looks that drastically, I guess. I'm not that daring."

At that, Tara broke in. "Good grief, Hope," she complained. "You sound as if Olivia's robbed a bank or something. What's so drastic about plucking your eyebrows?"

"*I* say, if it feels right to you, then go with it," she added, addressing Olivia.

But it was Duffy's reaction that confused Olivia most of all. In theory, Duffy had accepted her decision that they should let their relationship cool off. In practice, it seemed that Duffy just happened to be around almost every day to offer her a ride home from school. Duffy had a way of ignoring unpleasant realities, which Olivia found hard to deal with. And he seemed just as determined to ignore her efforts to change her image.

When he picked her up after school, he didn't comment on her new look one way or another. He just drove along, whistling the tune playing on the radio.

"So, what do you think?" she challenged him.

"About what?" he asked. As if he didn't know.

"What do you think? The new me."

They pulled up to a red light, and Duffy turned to study her, as if this were the first time he'd noticed the change. "I don't know," he said finally. "I was partial to the old Olivia. So I guess I'm not the best person to ask."

"Well, Hope likes it," she stated defiantly. "So does Tara."

"Okay."

Olivia recognized that special tone of voice that Duffy used when he found himself interviewing some nut case for the *Tarenton Lighter*. "I was invited to go for a ride in a flying saucer," the source would tell Duffy. "And guess what? The creatures from outer space looked like golden retrievers!"

And Duffy would say "okay" in that same noncommittal way.

"You can't get away with that," she said. "I'm not some stranger that you're talking to for the paper. This is me, Olivia."

Duffy whistled again. "Could have fooled me."

"Don't tease!" Olivia was so frustrated that her eyes filled with tears. Automatically, she put her hand to her eyes to wipe them, realizing too late that she would just be smearing her mascara. Now her left eye was stinging a little, and she probably looked a mess.

"Hey, it's nothing to cry about." They had just turned onto Main Street and Duffy pulled into a parking space and took her in his arms. "You know I'm crazy about you, whatever you do. I just don't see the need for all these changes. Everything was going so great until Walt came back to town."

"This has nothing to do with Walt!" Olivia

protested, though she wasn't entirely sure that was true. "Don't you see? I'm not ready to accept that my life is just going to go forward in a straight line from now on. I need to find out who I really am."

Duffy gave her a supportive hug. "Okay. Of course I understand. I just want you to know my feelings for you won't change a bit."

The conversation was interrupted by agitated tapping on the car window on Olivia's side. She and Duffy looked up to see Mrs. McCready, the owner of the yarn and knitting supplies store they were parked beside, motioning wildly with her hands.

"No smooching in front of my store," fussed Mrs. McCready. "No smooching here. It's bad for business. You kids should be ashamed of yourselves."

"Of course, ma'am," Duffy said, his face a mask of sincerity. "We'll move right away. And we *are* ashamed. We promise we'll never smooch near a yarn store again."

"Good. I'm glad you've learned your lesson!" Mrs. McCready said, caught off balance by Duffy's apology.

Olivia was biting her lower lip, nearly bursting with the effort to keep a straight face. Duffy started the engine and they got away fast.

"Smooching!" Olivia whooped, as soon as they were safely away. "I didn't want to laugh in her face, but that's such a *quaint* word."

Duffy smiled halfheartedly. "Poor Mrs. McCready," he said in a voice heavy with self-pity.

"That's what happens to those of us who don't change with the times. We become obsolete."

It wasn't until an hour or so later, when she was in her room trying to study, that Olivia realized that she'd let Duffy win another round. Instead of impressing him with the "new Olivia," she'd ended up reverting to the role of sweet little Livvy. She was so frustrated that she picked up the foam rubber pillow from her bed and threw it at the wall. But just like Duffy, the pillow bounced back and landed at her feet.

CHAPTER

"All right girls, vat vas it you wanted to know?"

Olivia shot Tara a look of reproach. The two of them were sitting in Madame Magda's living room, which looked a lot spookier than it had the first time Tara saw it. The shade of the lamp next to Madame Magda's chair had been draped with an embroidered shawl, which cast eerie, speckled shadows on the walls and ceilings. A stick of incense — Tara thought it must be sandalwood — was burning in a brass incense holder on the mantel.

Madame Magda herself was wearing a multi-colored silk scarf tied around her head, turban-style. When Tara and Olivia showed up on her doorstep, she had apologized for the scarf, explaining that she'd just washed her hair. But Tara couldn't help thinking that it made the psychic look like a carnival fortune-teller.

Olivia was sorry that she'd ever let Tara talk her into coming along. Although she'd told herself that she was only doing it to keep Tara company, she'd been secretly hoping that Madame Magda might be able to give her some advice, too. Now she felt foolish.

"I don't have a problem," Olivia said finally. "I mean, it isn't exactly a problem."

"Iz zat so?" Madame Magda looked at her in polite disbelief.

"She does too have a problem," Tara put in. "She has two boys who like her, and she can't decide which one to choose."

"That's not true!" Olivia protested. "I don't want to choose either one. It's just that they can't seem to accept that. I keep telling Duffy I want to cool it, but he acts as if he doesn't hear me."

"And the other young man?" Madame Magda asked.

"His name is Walt," Olivia said. "We were together once. Now we're seeing each other again. But he doesn't want me to date other guys. Just him."

Madame Magda shook her head sorrowfully. "Zis is too bad. But I can't tell you vat to do. I give no advice."

So why are we here? Olivia wondered.

"I'm sorry we bothered you then," she said. "I guess we'd better be going."

"Vait, Vait. Not so fast." Madame Magda

reached across the coffee table and took Olivia's hand in her own. "I have no advice. But sometimes I see things. Maybe I help you a little."

Madame Magda's eyes were closed now. Olivia wanted to get out of there, but her wrist was being held firmly in Madame's grip. She made a face for Tara's benefit, but to her surprise, Tara seemed to be taking all this completely seriously.

"Ah, now I see," Madame Magda said. Her voice was low, almost hoarse, and she seemed to be talking to herself. "I see Olivia with a rose behind her ear. I see her dancing. Dancing and happy. Yes! Very happy!"

Madame's eyes snapped open.

"Wow!" Tara was practically speechless, she was so impressed. Olivia could hardly believe how gullible Tara was.

"Thank you," Olivia told Madame Magda. "I mean, it's nice to know that you think I'm going to be happy. Even if it doesn't make me any less confused right now."

"Don't worry, my dear," Madame told her. "Ven ze time is right, you vill no longer be confused. You vill know whom you should choose."

Olivia started to get up, but Madame had taken hold of Tara's hand and was staring blankly in the general direction of the ceiling. "Such a strong aura you have," she told Tara. "I see it over your head now. A violet aura. Zees is very special."

"It is?" Tara was thrilled.

Madame shut her eyes again. "I see you making a journey. A journey with friends. People are

40

running. Young men in suits with numbers on them. They are playing a game."

"Right," agreed Tara breathlessly. "A basketball game, I bet. We have an exhibition game coming up next week with Danville. It's pretty far away. That must be the journey you're seeing."

Madame Magda showed no signs of hearing Tara's chatter. Her mouth was twisted in a pained grimace. "Zees is bad, very bad," she croaked. "I see trouble. A difficult journey. I see an animal. An animal with big teeth. . . . No, wait! . . ."

Madame Magda let out a low, mournful wail. The sound was so unlike her normal voice that even Olivia was starting to get spooked.

There was a long silence, then Madame Magda shrieked, "I see a devil! A devil with a forked tail. I see something slick! Then a crash . . ."

Madame's eyelids popped open, and her body relaxed. She looked drained and a little breathless.

"What does it mean?" Tara begged. "Does it mean something terrible is going to happen?"

Madame shook her head. "Try not to worry, my dear. Sometimes my visions are strange. Perhaps it means nothing at all."

Five minutes later, Tara and Olivia were back in Tara's gold Chevy, on their way to Olivia's house.

"I have to admit it," Olivia laughed nervously, "your Madame Magda really had me going there for a minute. That was a pretty good show she put on."

41

"A show!" Tara gasped. "Is that what you think it was?"

"I sure do," Olivia said. "Don't tell me you take all that devil stuff seriously. She was just trying to scare us."

"I don't think so. I think she's sincere."

"What about that stuff about you having an aura?" Olivia reminded her. "I hadn't noticed any violet clouds around your head lately."

"So? You're not psychic. Of course *you* wouldn't see it."

"Besides," Tara added, "I don't see how you can accuse her of wanting to scare us when she told us to forget about what she said."

"Sure she did. But who could forget a prediction like that?"

"Well, that's not Madame Magda's fault."

Olivia shrugged. It was a waste of time arguing with Tara when she started using her own special brand of logic. "You can take all this seriously if you want to," she told Tara. "But I think it's a big joke. And I don't intend to waste one minute of my time worrying about nonsense like that."

Olivia kept her promise so well that by practice the next afternoon she wasn't thinking about Madame Magda at all. "I still haven't figured out a special routine for the Danville game," she told the group after they had finished their warm-ups. "But in the meantime, let's try the new lead-in for the fight song."

The cheerleaders lined up, one behind the

other, with Peter and Sean at the rear, holding megaphones.

Hope, at the front of the line, started the chant:

"WE'VE GOT THE SPIRIT," she yelled, then peeled off to the left in a cartwheel, ending in a split.

"WE'VE GOT THE ZING," shouted Olivia, doing the same maneuver to the right.

"WE'VE GOT THE PRIDE," shouted Jessica, spinning off to the right.

"SO COME ON, LET'S SING," Tara yelled, finishing up with a cartwheel to the left.

Sean and Peter remained to lead off the song:

> "Three cheers for Tar-en-ton,
> Hooray for Tar-en-ton,
> The pride of every student here . . ."

Unfortunately, Sean was not a singer at all. His voice was loud and strong but slightly off pitch. Peter struggled valiantly to lead Sean back to the right notes, but Sean didn't realize that he was wandering from the melody until he hit a real clunker.

"Stop, I'm begging you." Jessica sank to her knees and raised her hands in mock horror.

"I guess I was a little off," Sean admitted cheerfully.

"A little!" Jessica exclaimed. "I don't think this is going to work. We'd better put someone who can carry a tune at the back of the line."

"But Sean is so tall," Olivia pointed out. "It won't look right if he's near the front."

"You'll just have to learn to sing, Dubrow," Peter informed Sean. "Anyone can learn if they really want to. Even you."

"What's that supposed to mean? 'Even me'?" Sean shot back. "I'm not that bad."

It was a good-natured argument, but Tara was getting more agitated by the second. "How can you two squabble over something so unimportant!" she snapped at them. "We shouldn't even be going to the Danville exhibition game. It's too dangerous."

Everyone stared at her. "What do you mean, dangerous?" asked Hope.

Tara explained about Madame Magda vision. "Don't you see? It must mean that we're going to get into an accident on the way to the game. There'll be something slick on the road, then a crash."

Coach Ardith Engborg had been listening from a seat in the front row of the bleachers. "That will be quite enough," she told Tara. "I plan to drive the squad to Danville in the school minibus. You don't have to come with us if you don't want to. Melissa can cheer in your place. But I won't have you scaring the rest of the squad with these foolish superstitions."

"This isn't a superstition," Tara protested. "It was a vision. Don't you understand? I'm trying to save us all from danger."

Coach Engborg looked grim. "In my book, it's superstition. No one can predict the future. I realize a lot of people enjoy that kind of thing, but I don't. And I don't want to hear another word about it during practice."

"But this is important," Tara insisted. "Madame Magda said . . ."

The coach interrupted by gesturing toward the door with her thumb. "I don't care what Madame Magda said. I said, one more word and you're out, and I meant it. You can resume practicing with the squad when you're ready to promise me that you won't discuss this again."

Tara couldn't believe this was happening. She wasn't sure she really believed in Madame Magda's vision enough to stay away from the game. But surely she was right to want to warn the group. Why was the coach being so unreasonable?

Sulky and unrepentant, she picked up her gear and marched off to the locker room. If the coach wanted it that way, fine. She could be stubborn, too.

The rest of the cheerleaders knew that saying anything now would only make Coach Engborg dig in her heels. No one said another word about Madame Magda until practice was over and the coach was back in her office with the door shut behind her. Then everyone gathered around Olivia to hear the details.

Sean couldn't stop chuckling over the part about Tara's violet aura. "The person who told her that was really a con artist," he laughed. "Tara loves to be special. It isn't enough that she's a great-looking girl with a fantastic figure. She has to have an aura, too. Now I've heard everything."

Melissa looked unhappy. "Naturally, I'll be ready to cheer at the Danville game," she said, "but I hate to have it happen this way. Tara looked awfully upset."

"Don't worry about Tara," Olivia told her. "The coach told her she can come back whenever she's ready to stop spreading gloom and doom. If she doesn't agree to drop this whole subject, that's her problem."

Tara, however, was not ready to give up. After she left the school, she drove around Narrow Brook Lake several times, trying to figure out what to do next. She was sure that Madame Magda had special powers. But how was she ever going to convince the rest of the squad that they were in danger? Even Olivia, who had been right there when the psychic had made her prediction, refused to take it seriously.

There isn't a single person who believes me, Tara thought. Patrick thinks I'm out of my mind. Nancy Goldstein and Nick all but laughed in my face. The rest of squad will take Olivia's word over mine, no matter what I say.

That left just one solution. Somehow, she told herself, I'm going to have to find a way to keep the squad from going to the Danville game.

Now that she'd made her decision, Tara felt pleased with herself, but a little scared, too. Danville was only an exhibition game, so it didn't really matter whether the squad showed up or not. It certainly wasn't worth taking risks over. But how could she possibly keep the cheerleaders from going?

Tara drove around for almost an hour before she came up with a plan that just might work. The trouble was, she couldn't bring it off alone. If only she could find an ally — someone who was nervy and a good enough actor to fool the squad and Coach Engborg, too.

CHAPTER

After practice, Olivia caught a ride to the mall with Sean Dubrow. Sean was meeting his girlfriend, Kate Harmon, so that they could shop together for a birthday present for her father. Olivia decided to go along on the chance that she could see Walt at Carey's motorcycle shop, where he had been working since he took a leave of absence from college.

While he drove, Sean quizzed Olivia about her love life. "What's going on with you and Walt?" he asked her.

Olivia sighed. "You mean, what isn't going on. Not a whole lot recently."

"I don't get it. When Walt came back to Tarenton, I thought he was determined to win you back from Duffy. And it seemed to me that he had just about succeeded."

"That was before he realized that I was determined to keep on seeing Duffy, even if only as a friend," Olivia explained. "Walt found out that Duffy drove me home from school a couple of times, and he was upset. He just can't accept that things have changed. He wants us to be together one hundred percent or not at all, I guess."

It struck Olivia as strange that she should be confiding all this to Sean Dubrow of all people. Sean was probably the handsomest guy in the senior class, tall and broad-shouldered, a real hunk. But until he met Kate Harmon, Sean had played the field, dating half the girls at Tarenton High and leaving a trail of broken hearts behind while he moved on, without so much as a backward glance. Sean had never meant to hurt any girl's feelings. It just didn't occur to him that other people took emotional involvements more seriously than he did. But Olivia had never approved of the way Sean ran his act.

Now, though, she was starting to feel some sympathy for Sean's former ways. "Why does Walt have to be so stodgy about this?" she complained. "You must understand why I'm in no hurry to go back to the relationship we had last year."

"I do see how you feel," Sean sympathized. "But I guess I also see how Walt feels. Now that Kate and I are together, I don't think I could stand to share her with anyone."

This wasn't what Olivia wanted to hear. "It seems to me that the old double standard is at work here," she complained.

"How so?" Sean asked. "I mean, Walt isn't seeing anyone else. Is he?"

"No, that's not it. But when he wanted to go away to work last summer, before going to college, he didn't feel he owed me any apologies. Now he comes waltzing back, and he thinks I'm going to be ready to erase all the changes I've made in my life and go back to where we were last year."

Sean looked baffled, and Olivia didn't entirely blame him. Sometimes it amazed her that she still couldn't forgive Walt for taking that summer theater apprentice job, leaving home — and her — three whole months before he had to go away to college. He had even expected her to be thrilled that he had the opportunity. So far, though, she hadn't found anyone who understood how she felt. The rest of the world seemed to assume that on graduation day, all bets were off. Couples split up and went their separate ways, and no one thought a thing about it. Maybe it was because she had been just a junior, left behind while Walt and all her senior friends were going off to start a new phase of their lives, that she had been so hurt.

"I hate to say this," Sean said finally. "But you might have to accept the possibility that you and Walt can't work this out. I mean, you want one thing right now and he wants another. Sometimes there's no way to compromise."

"Thanks a lot," Olivia told him. "That really cheers me up."

*   *   *

When they got to the mall, Kate was waiting at the entrance to Stanley's department store, and she and Sean went off arm in arm in the direction of the men's department. Olivia, left alone, went down the escalator to the lower promenade, where Carey's cycle shop was located.

Walt was standing near the big display window, showing a cycle to a couple who had two children with them, one a toddler and the other an infant in a papooselike carrier. Olivia stood outside for a while, watching. Walt seemed so confident, so in control. Although the customers were at least ten years older than him, they were treating him as an equal. Walt looked good, too. His compact shape looked leaner and more muscular. Even his face looked more mature since he had started to wear his hair a little longer.

Common sense told her that Sean was right. She couldn't turn back the clock. Maybe she should just accept that her relationship with Walt was changed, maybe beyond patching up. But seeing Walt like this, she felt as close to him as ever. So much for common sense.

She waited until he had finished talking to the young couple, then walked by the store, pretending to "accidentally" notice Walt, who was standing just inside the door. He immediately came out and greeted her with a hug.

"Hey there, Livvy. You look . . . you look different."

Not great. Not good. Just different.

Olivia sighed. "You're tough to impress. You really are."

"No I'm not." Walt flashed a disarmingly innocent grin. "I'm easy. Just try me."

Olivia had been sure that if she just had a chance to see Walt face to face, he would ask her out on another date. When he showed no signs of doing that as they talked, she had to be the one to make the suggestion. "There's a school holiday tomorrow," she reminded him at last. "Maybe we could do something together."

"Sorry, I really am. But I have to work tomorrow evening."

"How about in the afternoon?" Olivia persisted. "We could go to a movie. Or I could come over to your place to see some tapes." Walt's parents had worked for the local TV station before moving to New York and bigger things, and Walt had always had more video equipment and more tapes than some stores. When he'd moved back to his aunt Helene's house in Tarenton, he'd had all his equipment shipped to him.

"Okay. But what about David Duffy?"

"Well, I'm not inviting him." Olivia said, trying to make a joke of it.

"I mean, I want to know where I stand."

"Wait a second. You're the one who left town last summer, not me. And I'm not saying that we can pick up where we left off. This is just a date."

She half expected Walt to say "Forget it." Instead, he just shrugged. "Fine. If that's the way you want it."

"Good. You know, maybe you could help me figure out a routine for the squad to do at the Danville exhibition game. You came up with such a good idea last time. And I'm really dense when it comes to thinking up things like that."

Suddenly, Walt's mood changed. He scowled. "I get it. You don't really want to see me. You just want me to bail you out by coming up with a routine. What's the matter? Can't Duffy think of anything?"

"Wait! That's not fair! That isn't why I want to see you."

Olivia was indignant. How could Walt think that she cared more about a dumb routine than about him? She knew, though, that it hadn't been a very tactful moment to ask for a favor. So why had she said it? Honestly, she wasn't sure. The words had just come rushing out.

Walt looked as if he had a lot more to say, but they were interrupted by the arrival of Hope's friend, Tony Pell. Tony already owned a motorcycle, but he stopped by Carey's frequently, just to check out the new models and talk to the salespeople.

When he saw Olivia, Tony brightened. "Hey, girl, you look fabulous," he said. "That's really a bad image. Bad in the sense of good, I mean."

Olivia glowed. Tony was the first person to really appreciate her new look. True, Tony wasn't the person she'd normally seek out for advice on style. Though no one called him "Tough Tony" anymore, he still dressed in oil-stained jeans, T-shirts with slogans for garages and car products, and a well-worn leather bomber jacket.

But Tony also happened to be very handsome. His long eyelashes and deep blue eyes were dreamy. Besides, Tony liked Hope, so no one could accuse him of having bad taste in girls.

Olivia waited around for a few minutes while Tony asked Walt questions about a new motorcycle suspension on one of Carey's models. But Walt's actions had made it clear that he was in no mood to continue their conversation. When he finished talking to Tony, he turned his back and headed off to help another customer.

"Am I wrong, or is Walt giving you the cold shoulder?" Tony asked.

"You're not wrong. We just had a disagreement."

"Don't be too hard on him," Tony advised. "He has a lot of changes to get used to. Before he was a senior cheerleader, a big wheel. And you were 'little Livvy,' right? It's not that way anymore. I mean, now you have all the power."

Olivia hadn't thought about it that way before. "The trouble is, I'm not sure whether I want to have power," she told Tony. "There are too many decisions to make."

"Well, yeah." For that matter, Tony wasn't sure he liked giving advice to the lovelorn. He wasn't used to playing that role, and it made him uncomfortable.

Impulsively, Tony walked over to the flower-seller's cart that stood in the middle of the mall promenade. He fished into his jacket pocket, pulled out a dollar, and plunked it down under the nose of the startled vendor. Then he selected a single pink rose, snapped off the stem, and tucked the flower behind Olivia's ear.

54

"There," he said, studying the result. "That looks nice. Now you've got to smile. Right?"

Olivia smiled a bit guiltily. "Thanks, Tony. You're sweet."

Tony looked mortified. "Well, yeah," he mumbled. "But I gotta go now. I'm meeting Hope."

It wasn't until after Tony had left, that Olivia remembered Madame Magda's prediction: "I see Olivia with a rose behind her ear."

She shivered. This was getting spooky.

All that evening, Olivia tried to tell herself that the rose was a coincidence. How could Madame Magda possibly have known Tony would do that? Tony didn't know himself he was going to do it until it actually happened.

Since she couldn't come up with an explanation, she decided that the best thing to do was just forget about the whole incident. If she could.

CHAPTER

Jessica Bennett rolled over in bed and opened one eye. The room was light, suspiciously light for six-thirty in the morning. Tentatively, she peeked at the clock alarm. The bright blue digital numbers fairly screamed at her: 8:15.

"Good grief!" she grumbled. She was late. Exploding into action, she jumped out of bed, grabbed a skirt and sweater from her closet, and sprinted to the bathroom. On her way, she noticed the open door of her mom and Daniel's bedroom. Both of them were gone, and the bed was neatly made.

Why hadn't her mother made sure she was up before she left for work?

Of course, she was too old now to expect her mother to wake her in the mornings. But since Mom insisted on doing it anyway, Jessica had come to depend on her. Now, it seemed, her mother was changing the rules without warning. Jessica felt annoyed and a little bit neglected, too.

Dressing in record time, she ran into the kitchen, where she found Daniel, her stepfather, peacefully having his morning cup of tea and a doughnut.

"Can you drive me to school?" she asked breathlessly.

Daniel chewed his last bite of doughnut thoroughly and turned the page of his morning paper before answering. "I *could*. But I don't think it would be a good idea."

Jessica frowned. What did he want her to do? Beg?

"Please, Daniel," she said. "I missed the bus, and now I'm late. And I really can't afford to miss French. I've got enough problems in that class already."

"You won't miss it." Daniel was smiling now, in that peculiar smug way that Jessica found so infuriating.

"Okay," she said, giving up. "What's the joke?"

"There's no school today. Remember? The teachers have State Conference, so you kids get the day off."

"Oh. Right." Jessica collapsed into the nearest chair.

"You don't look very happy about it," Daniel observed. "I should think that an extra day off would be a big deal. I mean, at your age, you shouldn't have any trouble thinking of things to do with your time."

Daniel selected another doughnut, bit off a chunk, and went back to reading the sports page. Jessica tried counting backwards from a hundred. Anything to stifle her impulse to strangle him with her bare hands.

In her calmer moments, Jessica knew that Daniel was not really a bad guy. He was loving to her mom and, from time to time, he even went out of his way to do nice things for Jessica. It wasn't his fault that he could never take the place of her real father.

Still, Daniel did have a knack for saying the wrong things. Ever since she had broken up with Patrick, Jessica hadn't quite known what to do with her free time. All her friends seemed to be paired off with someone, and if she went anywhere alone she was sure to run into Patrick and Tara together.

"If you really don't have anything to do," Daniel said, "I can make some suggestions."

That was another one of Daniel's annoying habits, reading her mind, Jessica thought. When she didn't answer, he reminded her that she had hardly used the set of audio tapes he'd bought to help her with her French. And she could always do a few loads of laundry.

"And this evening," added Daniel, "your mother and I are going to visit my folks. You haven't seen them in weeks."

Jessica sighed. Daniel's parents meant well, but they treated her as if she were about eight years old. They were always giving her strange presents, too. One time they had given her a costume doll dressed up like a Southern belle. When Jessica opened the package she must have looked puzzled because Daniel's father explained, "It's Scarlett O'Hara, from the movie *Gone With the Wind*. I guess you young folks don't know that movie anymore. A real classic." Of course, Jessica did know the movie. Who didn't? She just wasn't interested in having a Scarlett O'Hara doll. But Daniel's parents didn't take the hint. They never did.

Jessica could see from the look on Daniel's face that there was no way of getting out of the visit without making a big scene. "Okay, I'll go," she said. "And I'll do some chores and study before dinner. But the rest of the day is mine."

Before Daniel could object, she left the table and hurried back to her room, where she changed into her running outfit and shoes. In five minutes she was out of the house.

Jessica didn't run for training, but because she liked the way running made her feel. For a little while, she could forget about all her problems and just coast along, concentrating on putting one leg ahead of the other.

Lithe and leggy, Jessica was a graceful runner. As she loped along Carey Avenue, the tree-lined street that led out in the direction of Lake Road, she kept up an easy stride.

At the intersection of Lake Road, she ran into another morning jogger, Peter Rayman. Peter had just done three miles, pushing himself hard all the way. His expression was serious, almost tense, and he probably wouldn't have noticed Jessica at all if she hadn't called out to him.

"I'll jog with you awhile," she said after they'd exchanged hellos. "But only if you slow down. I'm not into torturing myself."

Peter nodded his agreement and they started off. Jessica set the pace, and he matched her stride for stride. They were enjoying themselves so much, that they ran all the way to the little picnic area where the shore of Narrow Brook Lake could be seen from the road.

There was a broad, flat rock with a view of the lake, and for a few minutes they sat there, cooling down and enjoying the view. Peter didn't try to make conversation, and Jessica liked that. Even though they'd hardly said a word, she felt their minds were very much in tune.

For that matter, she was starting to notice that Peter was attractive in other ways, too. He wasn't handsome and outgoing like Patrick or Sean Dubrow, but he had strong, wiry muscles and an intense personality.

Even though they'd been on the cheerleading squad together all year, Jessica realized that there was a lot she didn't know about Peter. Maybe the time had come to get to know him better. . . .

Just as Jessica's thoughts started to get interesting, they were interrupted by the loud honking of a car horn. She and Peter turned to see Tara Armstrong at the wheel of her gold Chevy. Tara had seen them from the road and stopped to say hello. "Isn't it great to have a day off," she cried happily. "I love it. We're going over to Grove Lake to play some tennis."

60

Peter and Jessica exchanged annoyed looks. Their quiet mood was completely shattered. They both noticed right away that the passenger in Tara's car was Diana Tucker, Tarenton High's professional troublemaker.

Diana was celebrating the day out of school by wearing her hair in an exaggerated style, combed and moussed into spiky peaks that stood almost straight up from the top of her head. Leaning out the passenger-seat window, she wasted no time in coming up with a catty remark.

"This is a pretty inconvenient place to come to make out," she said maliciously. "Isn't it awfully cold?"

"We didn't come here to make out," Peter snapped. "We were out jogging and we just happened to run into each other."

Diana was being nasty as usual. But Jessica wondered why Peter went out of his way to explain that she and he had met by accident. Did he guess what she had been thinking a few minutes ago? Was this his way of making sure she wasn't interested? Or was he just nervous about having Diana know his business?

Peter was the first boy Diana had tried to attract when she transferred to Tarenton High earlier in the year. Diana had caused trouble between Peter and Hope, his girlfriend at the time, and made him completely miserable before Peter finally figured out that she was only dating him to make trouble for the squad. After all that, Peter had good reason to dislike her.

Jessica wondered whether Peter wasn't secretly

a little bit hung up on Diana, even now. But Diana seemed determined to make Peter as miserable as possible. "You and Jessica don't have to keep any secrets from me," she teased him. "I imagine its tough to find places to go. Especially when you don't have a car."

That was the ultimate dig. Peter was sensitive about having no car and very little money.

"There are some people I wouldn't want to spend time with even if they had five cars," he told Diana.

Tara looked embarrassed. "Well, we could chat like this for hours," she said, exuding fake cheerfulness. "But Diana and I have a reserved court waiting for us."

She started the car, and Diana, ignoring Jessica completely, said good-bye to Peter. "Don't do anything I wouldn't do," she cooed.

"I can't imagine what that would be," Peter said sarcastically as the Chevy pulled away.

"Which makes me wonder what Diana is up to, playing tennis with Tara," he added. "I happen to know that she's a lousy tennis player, and Tara is a pretty good one."

"So? Maybe Tara is just giving her a lesson. You're too suspicious."

Peter shook his head. "Tara has been acting awfully strange ever since she got interested in that psychic. Now she's been kicked out of practice, and suddenly there's Diana Tucker hanging around with her. You can't tell me there's no connection."

Jessica reluctantly agreed. But she was in no

mood to waste the rest of her day off worrying about Tara Armstrong's problems. It was bad enough that Tara had Patrick. Why did she have to start making trouble for the squad, too?

As Peter predicted, Tara and Diana's tennis game didn't go very well.

Diana was not really interested in learning how to play, and even though Tara kept hitting easy balls to her, Diana missed more returns than she made. Sometimes she hardly tried to hit the ball at all. Instead, she'd make a little stab with her racquet and squeal "Oops!"

"You'd do better if you'd keep your eye on the ball instead of on the guys playing in the next court," Tara said disgustedly.

"But the guys on the next court are a lot more interesting," Diana giggled.

The players on the next court were college students from Grove Lake, and once they noticed Diana watching them, they, too, forgot about the game. Soon they had given up serving completely and were standing on their court making loud comments.

"Look at that form!" one of them shouted as Diana tossed the ball up to serve and then pawed at the air with her racquet, missing the ball completely. Obviously, he wasn't referring to Diana's tennis form.

"Way to *move!*" yelled another as Tara tried to chase down a forehand volley.

Tara was used to getting this sort of thing. Her lush auburn hair and perfect figure seemed to encourage some guys to make nerds of themselves, trying to get her attention. Normally, she was good at dealing with loudmouths, too. But with Diana encouraging the guys by giggling and making eyes at them, there was no hope that they'd ever leave them alone.

Finally, Tara lowered her racquet in the middle of a point and walked off the court. "I give up," she told Diana. "This is impossible."

"I agree," said Diana innocently, as if her behavior had nothing to do with the problem. "Let's get out of here."

Tara was so discouraged that she almost forgot about her reason for inviting Diana to play tennis in the first place. But later on, when they stopped at Benny's for a hamburger, Tara brought up the subject of Madame Magda, and Diana suddenly became a very good listener.

"Of course I believe in psychics," she said eagerly. "There was one out in California, where I went to school last year, who could tell you all about your previous incarnations. You know, your past lives. I went to see him once, and he told me in my former life I was burned at the stake as a witch."

"Smart man," said Tara.

But Diana was oblivious to the put-down, as usual. And Tara was so happy to be talking to someone who didn't think she was crazy, that she started to forget that she didn't especially trust or like Diana. Soon she told her the whole story of Madame Magda's prediction about the Danville game. "I'm just sure that if the squad goes to that game they'll be in an accident," she sighed. "But no one takes me seriously. I just wish there were some way to keep them home."

"That wouldn't be easy." While Diana considered the problem, she was chomping down on the last of a double order of greasy French fries. Tara watched enviously, making note of the fact that Diana had clear skin and a completely flat stomach.

After swallowing the last bit of fries, Diana started to come up with some wild ideas for stopping the game from taking place. "We could try kidnapping the entire basketball team," she suggested wildly. "You know, lure them one by one to some out-of-the-way place. And keep them there until after the game."

"Great," laughed Tara. "But how would we keep them from leaving? Tie them up?"

"We could always give them sleeping pills," Diana said. "But I don't know where we'd get any. My stepmom used to take them, but she quit. So maybe we could just lock them up somewhere. You know, one of us could ask each of the players to meet us in this place. Then when the guy showed up, he'd find all his friends there. If we thought of a good enough story to fool them with, they might be so embarrassed that they wouldn't even tell on us."

"I wouldn't count on it." Tara was still laughing, but she was starting to feel a little bit nervous, too. It was hard to be sure when Diana was kidding. "Anyway, I think that's a little extreme. Kidnapping could get us into a lot of trouble."

"I suppose," Diana conceded reluctantly. "If

you're too chicken to try that, we could always try hiding the cheerleaders' uniforms. Coach Engborg is such a stickler for appearances that she'd cancel the trip rather than let the squad appear in their street clothes."

Tara felt the mouthful of hamburger she was trying to chew go dry and tasteless. "I couldn't do that," she said in a shocked tone of voice. "That would be sabotaging the squad."

Diana shrugged. "What if you don't do it, and the squad gets into a terrible accident? It would be all your fault for not stopping them. You'd really feel guilty then."

Tara felt trapped. Say what you want about Diana, her logic made sense. "Okay," she said finally, "let's think up something. But not hiding the uniforms. Let's think of some way to convince them that the trip to Danville will be too dangerous. Then they'll change their own minds about going."

Diana reached for the uneaten French fries on Tara's plate. "That seems like the hard way to do it, if you ask me. But maybe we can do something that will scare the squad into staying home Friday night."

She thought for awhile, then shrieked, "Whoa, I've got a great idea. You know that old wolf suit that Sean wore when the squad did that skit for the pep rally earlier in the year? Is it still around?"

"I guess so," Tara said. "But so what? What good will that do us?"

"Maybe a lot," Diana promised her. "The idea

I've got is a little farfetched. But it just might work. Everyone's a little bit superstitious, even Coach Engborg, who pretends to be above it all. Listen . . ."

Diana was so excited about her plan that you could almost see the wheels turning in her brain as she worked out the details. "After we're finished with our little show," she concluded, "the squad will be so scared that they won't *dare* leave for Danville."

CHAPTER

8

Sean Dubrow and Kate Harmon were spending their day off at the mall. Kate still hadn't been able to find a birthday present for her father, and she was starting to feel desperate.

"I don't see why we're making such a big deal out of this," groused Sean for about the fiftieth time that afternoon. "If it were my dad, I'd just get him a sweater. Or a shirt."

"That's what everyone gives him," Kate said. "My father must have a whole bureau full of shirts and sweaters he's never worn."

"So let's get him a record."

Kate shook her head. "He only likes classical music, and he's very picky."

"Okay. How about a book? Or a magazine subscription?"

"Uh-uh. He's got stacks of magazines that he doesn't have time to read."

"Obviously, your father doesn't need anything," Sean concluded. "Therefore, let's just get a nice card and forget about the present."

"I did that last year," Kate confessed. "That's one reason I feel extra obligated to get a special present this year."

Sean could hardly believe that he was wasting his school holiday trailing around the mall behind a girl. But then, it wasn't like Kate to make a major production out of shopping. Thin and angular, with frizzy hair and a complexion dusted with freckles, Kate was normally a whirlwind of efficiency. Since everyone deserved to be frazzled one in a while, Sean decided to go along with her.

"Okay, you win," he said. "We'll keep walking and see if we can think of a brilliant idea."

"Let's try the luggage section," Kate suggested. "Dad could use a briefcase. If I can find one I can afford to buy."

With Sean following behind her, Kate charged through the housewares and appliance section. "Look at the prices on this stuff," Sean joked. "I mean, who would spend a hundred dollars on a machine to chop onions with?"

"Maybe someone you know," said Kate, tugging his elbow to get his attention. Silently, she pointed to the next aisle, where Sean spotted his own father examining a huge avocado-colored refrigerator with double doors. With him was Marge Kopecki, a secretary at Tarenton Fabricators, whom his father had dated on and off for a few months.

"I don't get it," he whispered to Kate. "What

are Dad and Marge doing buying a refrigerator together?"

For a brief moment, Sean wondered if his dad and Marge were planning on getting married! If they were, they had done a good job of keeping their plans secret. As far as he knew, the two of them were just good friends.

"Let's get out of here," he said, practically dragging Kate backwards down the aisle.

He and Kate escaped through the nearest exit. Out on the mall promenade they stopped at a seating area filled with round tables and folding chairs, where shoppers could rest and eat food from the fast food restaurants located nearby. Kate found a table in a crowded section, out of sight of the exit, and sat down to catch her breath.

"I don't see why you're so worried about being seen," she complained. "There's probably some perfectly ordinary explanation. Maybe Ms. Kopecki is buying that refrigerator for herself and wanted your dad's advice."

"You haven't seen her apartment," Sean countered. "That refrigerator would never fit in her kitchen."

"Okay, so maybe your dad is buying it for your house."

"Without mentioning it to me? That's just my point. Why wouldn't he say something? Unless, he's getting married and hasn't bothered to mention the fact to his only son — or is keeping it a secret for some reason."

Kate frowned. "Would you really be so upset if your dad and Marge got married?"

Sean looked confused. "I don't know. I guess I just don't like the idea of being surprised. Dad and I have gotten along pretty well, just the two of us. Why wouldn't he tell me?"

Sean was still brooding when Jessica Bennett came out of Marnie's dress shop nearby and spotted them. "Mind if I join you?" she asked. "My mother has to work an hour overtime, so I'm stuck waiting for her. Then we're all going to visit Daniel's parents."

Jessica sat down and started giving them a rundown on her day so far. Her main complaint was Tara Armstrong. "I can live with the fact that she's dating Patrick," she grumbled. "But now she's causing trouble for the squad with all this psychic business. And hanging around with Diana Tucker, of all people. It just seems like no matter where I go, Tara pops up and ruins everything. Peter and I jogged all the way out to the lake, and we weren't there ten minutes before Tara and Diana came by, and of course Diana started making catty remarks."

"What kind of catty remarks?" Kate wanted to know.

"Oh, you know. Diana assumes that anytime a boy and girl are alone together that means that something is going on. It never occurs to her that you could just be friends. That girl is really a bad influence."

"Speaking of bad influences," Sean said, "what about that Madame Magda woman? I'd like to tell her to leave Tara alone."

"Why don't we then?" suggested Kate. "She's

giving a demonstration right here at the mall this afternoon. In fact, it starts in a few minutes. I saw the sign when we came in."

Sean slapped the table decisively. "Why not? Let's go down there and check out her talk. Then we'll confront her and make her admit she's a fraud."

Madame Magda's speech was scheduled for the small auditorium just down the promenade from where they had been sitting. When Sean, Kate, and Jessica arrived, most of the seats were filled. Soon Madame Magda arrived, dressed in a plain navy-blue suit.

"I can't explain why I have been granted my special powers," Madame Magda told the audience. "I don't understand it myself. But I can tell you that the spirit world is best treated with respect."

Someone in the back row made a rude noise. Madame Magda paused and pointed to the heckler. "For example. You, young man have very troubled aura. Gray and muddled. I see that you have suffered from pains in your back."

The heckler stopped grinning and nodded reluctantly, admitting that he did.

"That's ridiculous," whispered Kate. "Lots of people have back pains at one time or another. Especially if they're as overweight as that guy. You can just tell from the way he's sitting that he's uncomfortable."

"It's too bad Madam M. can't see my aura,"

Sean whispered back. "Right now, I bet it's bright red."

After a few minutes, Madame Magda asked the audience to send up small personal items so that she could "read" them for clues to the owner's thoughts.

Sean immediately fished into his pocket and came up with his Swiss Army knife. "Let's call her bluff."

"Not me," Kate said. "Why play into her hands? I'm not giving that woman a chance to play games with my mind."

Jessica hesitated. She thought Kate was right, sort of, but when Madame Magda's assistant came up the aisle, she impulsively reached into her purse and handed him a small monogrammed compact.

When the audience's contributions were delivered, Madame Magda spread them out on the table next to the podium. Closing her eyes, she waved her hands over the objects, then zeroed in on Sean's pocketknife.

"All *right,*" whispered Sean. Leaning back in his chair, he waited confidently for Madame M. to make a fool of herself.

Madame Magda held the knife in her hand for almost a minute. "I see . . . I see a young man worried about a relationship," she began. "He is thinking about marriage. Wondering if it would be a good idea."

The grin on Sean's face dissolved.

Madame Magda looked out at the audience,

shielding her eyes with her hand. "Is the owner here? Can he tell me whether I am right?"

Reluctantly, Sean spoke up. "Pretty close," he acknowledged. He had just been thinking about marriage, in connection with his dad.

Jessica, impressed in spite of herself, was starting to feel sorry that she had ever handed over her compact. She watched anxiously as Madame Magda passed her hands over the pile of personal objects a second time and selected — her compact.

"Ah," cooed Madame. "Here we have an object that gives off many vibrations."

Kate nudged Jessica with her elbow and laughed. "Bet you didn't know your compact was giving off vibrations," she whispered.

"Shh," Jessica told her. This wasn't funny anymore. Not when it was her mind that was about to be read.

"The owner of this compact is a young girl," Madame continued. "A young girl in love. . . . Well, maybe not so much in love. She is attracted, but she has yet to make up her mind. Let me see now if I can visualize the young man's name."

Madame Magda pressed her fingers to her forehead. "It begins with the letter P. Let me see now. Not Paul. Not Prentice. It's Peter! Yes, that's it." She scanned the audience again. "Am I right? Will the young lady who owns the compact please stand and tell the audience whether I have spoken the truth?"

Jessica felt herself blushing a bright red. Kate

and Sean were looking at her with quizzical expressions.

"Hey, Jessica," hissed Sean. "Is she right? Are you nursing a secret passion for Peter?"

Kate gave him a dirty look. "Give her a break."

By now, the whole audience had turned around in their seats and was staring in Jessica's direction. She had no choice but to stand up and acknowledge that she was the owner of the compact. "I do know someone named Peter," she admitted. "But I'm not in love with him."

As soon as the admission was out, she quickly sank back into the seat.

"But maybe you have a little crush on this young man. No?" persisted Madame Magda.

"No!" Jessica insisted.

She sounded so defensive that the whole audience burst out laughing.

"And when did you last see this Peter?" Madame Magda asked.

"Today," Jessica mumbled.

"What did you say? I didn't hear you." Madame Magda asked.

Jessica spoke up. "Today."

Once again, the audience erupted in condescending laughter.

Finally the embarrassing moment passed, and Madame Magda went on to "read" some of the objects sent up by other members of the audience. Jessica just wanted to escape from the room, but she couldn't even do that because she had to wait until the end of the presentation to get her compact back.

When the assistant returned their things and the meeting broke up, Kate glared at both Sean and Jessica with her "I told you so" look. "Didn't I warn you guys not to give that fraud a chance to play games with your heads?" she asked.

"I'm not sure she is a fraud," Sean said. "Personally, I was pretty impressed. And I sure learned something new about Jessica."

"But it's not true!" Jessica protested. "I told you that!"

"Oh, come on, Jessica," Sean teased. "Confess. There's nothing wrong with a little crush. I'm sure Peter wouldn't mind."

"Sean Dubrow! If you dare mention one word of this to Peter I'll never speak to you again."

"Ah, come on, can't you take a joke?"

"There's nothing funny about spreading stories that aren't true," Jessica told him. To herself, though, she had to admit that Madame Magda's prediction was pretty close to the mark. She had been thinking about Peter that way, even if it was just a passing idea.

"It is amazing, though," she said aloud. "I mean, how did Madame Magda come up with the name Peter? And that bit about you thinking of marriage?"

Kate groaned. "You two are really gullible. We were just talking about that stuff a few minutes earlier. Probably one of those assistants overheard us and passed the word to Madame Magda."

"Yeah, I guess so," Jessica said, without conviction. Kate's explanation made a certain amount of sense. But then, it was easy for Kate to be calm and rational. Madame Magda hadn't been revealing *her* secret.

CHAPTER

Olivia had made good use of her day off, and when cheerleading practice began the next afternoon she had a surprise announcement for the squad. "I've been working out a new halftime routine for the Danville game," she told them, "and we have a special guest today to help us learn the moves. This is Ms. Caroline Frazier, from the aerobics class that Melissa and I take at the Van Heusen studio. She's been nice enough to come over here to help us, so let's make her welcome."

The rest of the squad politely introduced themselves to Ms. Frazier, but not without exchanging a few doubtful glances. Their guest tutor was a slender, elderly lady wearing granny glasses and a lemon-yellow warm-up suit.

"I hope Olivia knows what she's doing," Sean whispered to Peter, as they pulled the mats onto the floor so the practice could get under way. "We only have this one practice to work out a routine, so there's not much time to waste on lectures from little old ladies."

Out on the floor, Ms. Frazier had already begun her talk. "Olivia invited me here because many years ago, back in the 1940s, I used to teach the jitterbug," she began. "She wanted me to explain some basic steps to you. But I think it will be easier just to show you the moves. Melissa here has already worked on some of this, so she'll be my partner."

Ms. Frazier turned to Olivia, who was operating the tape deck. "Okay, dear, any time you're ready."

Sean rolled his eyes in skepticism, and Hope Chang glared a warning.

Then the first cascading chords of music came pouring from the tape machine's speakers, and Ms. Frazier exploded into action. When it came to fast dancing, she was an expert, and Melissa could barely keep up. While the squad looked on in awe, she executed a series of fast-paced steps — jumping, twirling, and just plain boogeying, with one hand on her hip and the other pointing to the ceiling.

When the music ended, everyone applauded enthusiastically.

Ms. Frazier looked almost apologetic. "I left out the splits and the somersaults," she explained. "I'm afraid I'm not quite up to my old form. But I'll be happy to teach them to you if you're interested."

"We sure are," said Peter. "This is going to make a dynamite routine."

For the rest of the practice, Ms. Frazier took turns working with individuals and couples, demonstrating basic steps. In the meantime, the others tried out different ways of combining the jitterbug with basic cheerleading moves, like herkies, banana jumps, and flying fish. Since the jitterbugging included a lot of athletic partnering, with lifts and close footwork, the combination was natural. The main problem was to simplify the cheerleading moves enough so they could fit into the fast tempo.

By the end of the session they had worked out a good five-minute routine, beginning with some conventional cheers and then exploding into an exuberant dance.

"I don't know when I've had such fun," Ms. Frazier told them at the end of the session. She was barely breathing hard. "You kids aren't bad. For youngsters."

"We enjoyed it, too," Sean assured her. He was panting. "This is the best practice we've had in a while."

Olivia was feeling very pleased with herself. Why had she ever thought that she couldn't come up with new ideas? This one had occurred to her yesterday in exercise class when she saw Ms. Frazier demonstrating the jitterbug to some of the other members. She'd known right away that there was the basis of a routine. The hardest part had been getting up the nerve to present the idea to the group.

Coach Engborg was as happy as everyone else. "The routine certainly looks good," she told the squad. "And seeing Ms. Frazier is an inspiration. She's a wonderful example of the benefits of staying fit."

"That's for sure," said Melissa. "Ms. Frazier does aerobics every day. There are kids from Grove Lake High in the class, and some of them can't keep up with her."

"Speaking of other high schools," put in Hope. "How good is the Danville squad? None of us know anything about them since we don't normally play their school."

"That's a good question," said Coach Engborg. "All I know is that they have a coed squad. I haven't seen them for a while myself. It's been about five years since we played the Danville Devils."

"The who?" Sean and Jessica asked in unison.

"The Red Devils," Coach Engborg repeated. "That's what all the Danville teams are called. Have been for years. They even have a mascot who wears a devil suit with a tail. I think there have been a few protests from parents who don't appreciate the humor of the name. But it's been around a long time, and you know how people feel about tradition."

Sean looked thoughtful. "That's just what Tara said. Remember? That we would see a devil if we went to the game."

"Presented for your amusement," Peter intoned in his Rod Serling voice, "a town where devils play zone defense, and basketball players have cloven hooves."

"That isn't funny," Olivia protested.

"That goes double for me," Coach Engborg told him. "I told you once I don't want to hear any more jokes on this subject, and that rule is still in force."

In spite of the coach's warning, the whole squad gathered at the Pizza Palace after practice, and the subject inevitably came around to Tara and Madame Magda's visions.

"I don't suppose anyone's noticed that tomorrow is Friday the thirteenth," Sean said, as soon as they were gathered over a double-cheese pizza.

Jessica made a face. "I noticed it when I was filling out my appointment diary, but I decided it would be best not to say anything about it."

"Say anything about what?"

The question came from Patrick Henley, who had just come into the restaurant. He grabbed a can of Coke from the machine and sat down at the end of the long table.

Everyone started asking Patrick about Tara.

"We're not exactly on the outs," Patrick explained, "but I've hardly talked to her this week. She might as well be in outer space, considering how hard it is to communicate with her."

Olivia was in no mood for an update. She was still feeling euphoric from practice, and what she really wanted to do was talk to Walt. Now that the routine was all set, he couldn't accuse her of having an ulterior motive for wanting to see him, so it seemed the perfect time to call. Deserting her untouched slice of pizza, she went to the pay phone and dialed his aunt Helene's house. Walt answered on the first ring, and he sounded glad to hear from her.

"That sounds first-rate," he said, after she explained what the squad had worked out with Ms. Frazier. "I'd like to hear more about it. Why don't I come over now and we can talk?"

"Great," Olivia agreed. "See you in ten minutes or so."

When she got back to the table, Patrick was giving a one-man dramatic reenactment of the movie *Friday the 13th*. From there, he moved on to *Halloween* and *Nightmare on Elm Street*. Patrick had seen all the sequels — he could even recite all the plots without getting them confused.

"Actually," he summed up, "Tarenton is the kind of quiet, all-American town that these psycho villains like to haunt. It really makes you think. Don't you ever wonder whether some nerdy kid you teased in kindergarten, someone you've all completely forgotten, is going to come back to take his revenge on the senior class?"

David Duffy had arrived just in time to hear the end of Patrick's monologue. "I don't have to wonder," he said drily, "the nerdy kid I teased in kindergarten was you."

Everybody cracked up laughing, including Patrick. David borrowed a chair from a nearby table and sat down next to Olivia. He was wearing a trench coat and a battered Stetson hat. The outfit was straight out of a 1930s private eye movie, but somehow Duffy had the ability to wear clothes like that without seeming affected or silly.

Olivia thought he looked very romantic, but the timing of his arrival was terrible. Walt was going to show up any minute, and the first thing he would see when he arrived would be David Duffy, sitting right beside her. Olivia thought it over and decided that the best thing to do would be to leave the Pizza Palace entirely. She could wait outside for Walt and suggest they go somewhere else to talk. But when she got up to leave, Duffy stopped her.

"What's the matter," he asked. "You're not going because of me?"

"Not really," she lied. "I'm meeting someone."

"Walt, right?" guessed Duffy. "So why can't he come in here and meet you? I won't bite. I like Walt, as a matter of fact. There's no reason why we can't sit at the same table together."

"I know that...."

"But if that's the way you feel," he interrupted her, "I don't want to make trouble. I'll be happy to keep out of the way."

Dramatically, he replaced the hat he had removed when he sat down and moved to one of the corner tables, where he sat, leaning back against the wall, regarding the cheerleaders' table from under his pulled-down hat brim.

Olivia sighed. That was typical of Duffy. He might be out of the way, but he was hardly inconspicuous. She decided that she'd better leave anyway to head off trouble, but before she could say her good-byes, she saw that Walt was already parking his jeep in the lot, right in front of the big window.

Even though Patrick, Sean, and the others were eager to talk to him, it didn't take Walt fifteen seconds to spot Duffy. "What's Sam Spade doing here?" he demanded to know.

Duffy lifted his hat and regarded Walt thoughtfully. "It's a free country."

"Come on, Walt," said Olivia. "We don't have to stay here. Let's go."

Walt stared suspiciously at Duffy. "And if we do, is he going to be tailing us?"

It hadn't occurred to Duffy to do anything of the kind, but now that Walt had asked, he wasn't about to deny it. "It's a free country," he repeated.

Walt turned on his heel and walked out without another word. Olivia ran after him, but when they got outside Walt made it plain that he considered their date canceled. "I know you didn't plan this, Livvy," he told her. "But I just don't seem to fit into your life anymore. And David Duffy obviously does, since he's always around."

Olivia watched him go, wondering with whom she was more furious, Walt or Duffy. Her thoughts flew. Walt was certainly being inconsistent. If he really wanted to fit into her life, why did he get so touchy when she asked him to help her work on a cheerleading routine? As for Duffy, she'd had about enough of his games.

Going back inside, Olivia sat down at Duffy's

table. "You've got to give me a little space," she pleaded, trying to reason with him.

But Duffy just grinned. "I don't mean to make you unhappy," he said. "But you can't blame a guy for trying."

Yes, I can blame you, Olivia wanted to shout. Between the two of them, Walt and Duffy were driving her crazy. She wasn't even sure who she was anymore. She didn't know how to act, or even what she ought to look like.

She wanted to scream at Duffy, but she couldn't, not without most of the cheerleading squad and Patrick overhearing everything, and she didn't want to make a scene in front of them. As usual, Duffy had arranged things so that he would have the last word, and there wasn't a thing she could do about it. Yet.

CHAPTER

Jessica, for one, was finding it hard to sympathize with Olivia. Having two guys competing for her attention wasn't exactly the worst problem a girl could have. Lots of girls would be thrilled to be in Olivia's shoes. Anyway, Jessica had her own troubles having to get used to being around Patrick as a friend and getting over her jealousy of him and Tara. Yet the group assumed that good old Jessica could cope and gave Olivia their sympathy.

In fairness, Jessica didn't really blame Olivia. She didn't go out of her way to demand attention. But her petite size and big brown eyes made her friends feel that she needed protection. Jessica, on the other hand, impressed people as a happy person, cool and confident. Most of the time she liked having that image, but lately there were moments when she caught herself sinking into a swamp of self-pity. And tonight seemed destined to be one of those nights.

When she arrived home from the Pizza Palace there was a note from her mother and Daniel saying that they wouldn't be home until after midnight. She would have the house to herself all evening.

When she was still dating Patrick, the prospect of an evening home alone would have seemed like a luxury. Back then, she had always been pressed for time, trying to juggle schoolwork, cheerleading, and dating. Now, however, the unstructured hours loomed in front of her. She had already used the holiday to catch up on her homework and her chores, and it was already dark, too late for jogging.

Jessica fixed herself a chicken sandwich and a salad for dinner. Then she went to her room and sat down to read the book she was working on for her English term paper — *Jane Eyre*. In the story, the heroine becomes a governess at a huge old house in the English countryside. Its owner, Mr. Rochester, is a mysterious, romantic character.

Jessica had just come to the part about the madwoman living in the attic of Mr. Rochester's spooky old house. The idea was so creepy that it made Jessica shiver. She closed the book and tried to look at a magazine, hoping to rid her mind of the image. Instead, she found herself recalling the horror movies Patrick had described so vividly. Patrick loved movies like that, and when they were dating he had managed to talk her into seeing a few that she'd rather forget. To Patrick, the disgusting murder scenes were all a big joke, just special effects. He could laugh them off. She had always closed her eyes during the worst parts, but even so, she could hardly think about those movies without feeling a little bit queasy.

Patrick was right, though, she thought uneasily. Movies like that were almost always set in quiet, pretty, small towns, just like Tarenton.

No sooner had the thought crossed her mind than Jessica thought she heard footsteps crossing the cement patio just below her bedroom window. She looked out the window, but she couldn't see anything. It was dark out, and she had forgotten to turn on the floodlight that lit up the area between the back door and the garage.

Of course, the footsteps must have been in her imagination. She had just spooked herself by thinking about those awful movies. But as she started toward the door to the basement, where the floodlight switch was located, she heard another, louder, sound out in the backyard — a sort of muffled crash, like one of the patio chairs being knocked over.

Jessica looked for something to use as a weapon in case she needed to defend herself, but there was nothing nearby except a broom. That wasn't likely to do her much good, but she grabbed it anyway.

She was inching toward the light switch when she heard another sound, a sort of scrabbling noise just outside the kitchen window. Gathering all her courage, she looked around the corner, from the hall where she was standing, into the kitchen.

Then she saw it — a face, with huge, pointy teeth and a grinning mouth. It stared back at her for an instant, then it was gone, just as suddenly as it appeared.

Jessica opened her mouth to scream, but her throat was so dry that no sound came out. Then, feeling courageous all of a sudden, she flipped on the floodlight and ran to the window. But whatever it was that she had seen was gone — or else hiding out behind the garage, waiting for another chance to come after her.

She checked the door to make sure it was locked, then sat down at the kitchen table to collect her thoughts. She was sure she had seen something, or someone, but she wasn't really sure how to describe it. Her first thought was that it had been an animal. Maybe even a big dog. But any dog that could reach the kitchen window to look in, even standing on its hind legs, would have to be gigantic. Unreal. Bigger than any Great Dane she had ever seen.

Her second thought was that she had seen a person wearing some sort of elaborate mask. That was even scarier.

Her mother and Daniel had always emphasized that she should call the police right away if she heard a prowler when she was home alone. But the dispatcher who answered her phone call didn't seem to take her seriously.

"Are you sure what you saw wasn't a neighbor's dog?" the woman asked.

"I don't think so," Jessica insisted. "Besides, it looked kind of . . . I don't know, fake."

"Uh-huh," said the woman. "Can you be more specific?"

"I don't know. I only saw it for a second. Then it disappeared."

The dispatcher sounded weary. "I think your imagination is playing tricks on you, dear. But don't worry, I'll have the patrol car drive down your block and take a look around. In the meantime, you call back if you see anything else."

Jessica hung up in despair. Obviously, the woman didn't believe her. She was starting to feel more curious and angry than scared, and she felt tempted to go out and take a look around the backyard herself. But on second thought, that sounded a little bit foolish. Instead, she dialed Peter Rayman.

"I'll hop on my bike and come right over," he told her immediately. "You just sit tight until I get there."

Not ten minutes later, Peter arrived. He listened to Jessica's story, and then the two of them took a careful look around the backyard. They found no trace whatever of a prowler.

"I wouldn't blame you if you didn't believe me," Jessica told him. "The police dispatcher obviously thought the whole thing was my imagination or some kind of prank."

"Well, I believe you," Peter promised.

"There's probably nothing to worry about now, but I think I'll stick around until your folks get home, just in case."

Jessica brewed some mint tea, and the two of them settled down in the living room. They started to watch an old movie on TV, but before long Jessica started telling Peter about her family, especially her mixed feelings about her stepfather. "Daniel seems to think he has to make up for not being my real father by being twice as strict," she said. "Then he wonders why I resent him."

"Sounds tough," Peter agreed. "Still, there are lots of times I wish my mother had remarried. At least that way, I wouldn't feel so responsible. The way it is now, I can hardly win. If I want to go to college, it's going to be a big strain on my mother. Even with a scholarship and help from my dad, she'll end up having to work longer hours. On the other hand, if I don't go on to school, she'll be heartbroken. She's made so many sacrifices already, just to bring me up, that I'll feel guilty no matter what I do."

Jessica had never thought of what if must be like for Peter, who had no family at home except for his divorced mother. Maybe her problems weren't so bad after all.

She was also beginning to find out that there was a lot more depth to Peter than she had ever realized. He was such a private person that she had never realized how mature and thoughtful he was in many ways. Over the last few days, her image of him had changed drastically. Peter was a strong person. And interesting, too. For the first time, she could see why Hope had been attracted to him. Maybe she was starting to feel the same attraction. . . .

Peter interrupted her thoughts by getting up to refill his tea cup. "Sometimes I think I'll never get married," he said abruptly, almost angrily. "But believe me, if I do, it won't be for a long time. I don't plan to fall in love, either. It's too easy to get hurt."

Jessica was startled. "But what about Hope? I mean, not that the two of you were all that serious. But I always thought that you had special feelings for her."

"A case in point," Peter retorted. "Just about the time I started to get involved emotionally, our relationship turned sour. I don't plan to make that mistake again. I mean, I'll date. But I just won't lose control of my emotions."

Jessica felt stung. Of course, Peter's announcement hadn't been meant as a warning to her. At least, she didn't think it had. But she had just been letting herself imagine what it would be like to have Peter put his arms around her. For the second time in two days, she had felt that she and Peter were just seconds away from sharing a kiss.

This time, however, she couldn't blame an outsider for interrupting.

After Peter finished his second cup of tea, he set the cup down on the end table and moved a bit closer to Jessica. Casually, he rested his arm across the back of the couch. The tips of his fingers lightly brushed Jessica's shoulder.

Jessica could almost feel the buzz of electricity passing between them. All she had to do was move a few inches closer and they would be in each other's arms.

Her body was saying yes. But her brain was flashing an urgent warning signal. Why should she let herself get close to someone who had told her ahead of time that he had no intention of letting himself care for her?

It was tempting to think she could make Peter change his mind. But what if she were wrong? She would be taking all the emotional risks. And she would be the one to get hurt.

Jessica shook herself back to alertness, as if from a dream.

"Let's change the channel," she said, getting up to fiddle with the TV dials. "That show about the hospital is on tonight. You know, the one where the three doctors are all in love with the same patient. I want to see which one he ends up with."

To her relief, Peter didn't try to touch her again. Acting as if nothing at all had happened, he pretended to be wildly interested in seeing the latest episode of the hospital drama, and they were watching it together when Jessica's mother and Daniel showed up about half an hour later.

"The evening ended earlier than we expected," Abby Bennett said, as she took off her coat. "The McDougalls couldn't find a baby-sitter who could stay late."

"You didn't tell us you were having company," Daniel added, looking Peter over sharply, as if he were some sort of criminal.

Jessica explained that she'd heard a suspicious noise in the yard and Peter had been nice enough to come over to keep her company for the rest of the evening. She had been planning to tell them what she'd seen, but Daniel's behavior made her realize that he would never believe her, any more than the dispatcher at the police station had.

"Peter was really great to come to my rescue. But I'm sure the noise was just my imagination," she lied.

Fortunately, Peter didn't try to contradict her. He was an old hand at rearranging the details in ways that would keep his mother from worrying, so he caught on right away that Jessica was doing the same thing.

After that, Jessica walked him to the door to say good-bye, but Peter was in a hurry to get away. He knew that Jessica had very subtly rejected him, but he honestly wasn't sure why. It didn't occur to him that Jessica had been warned off by his speech about not getting emotionally involved. He was so afraid of being hurt himself that he didn't realize girls he liked might have the same fears.

Across town, at the all-night convenience store known as Bert's 24-Hour Shopper, Nick Stewart and Nancy Goldstein had stopped on their way home from a date so that Nick could fill his car's tank with gas. They had come inside the store to pay the cashier when they ran into Patrick Henley, who was on his way out, his pockets stuffed with candy bars and his hands clutching two bags of barbecue potato chips and a six-pack of root beer.

"Patrick, my man," said Nick heartily, clapping him on the shoulder. "Just the sight of you makes me want to buy stock in the junk food industry. So what if the rest of the population is transformed into health fanatics. You will single-handedly keep the candy makers in business."

"Candy alone wouldn't be so bad," put in Nancy, wrinkling her nose in distaste, "but who can eat chocolate and root beer at the same time? It's gross."

"I'll manage," Patrick assured her. "After all, I'm a growing boy." Drawing himself up to his full height, he flexed his biceps. After a year of working as a professional mover, even his lower arms had strong muscles. "Sometimes I wish my brain were as well developed," he said, only half joking. "You have no idea how much paperwork there is, even for a little business like mine. Bills to make out. Bills to pay. Accounts for the tax man. Tara was going to help me sort everything out, but we got into an argument over this psychic business and she walked out on me."

Nick frowned. "Don't tell me she's still riled up about that."

"More than ever," Patrick told him. "She's got this crazy idea about talking Coach Engborg into keeping the squad home from the exhibition game tomorrow night."

"That sounds like Tara," said Nancy. "She's so impulsive. I'm sure she absolutely believes that she's doing the right thing to save the squad."

"Impulsive is right," Nick echoed. "I may be the newest member of the Tarenton High faculty, but I think I know Coach Engborg well enough to understand that if there's one thing she has no sympathy for it's superstition. If Tara is spreading those kinds of ideas to the squad she could get them all in trouble."

Patrick listened to Nick with a sinking heart. Tara was so convinced she was right that there was no reasoning with her. But if she turned out to be wrong, and her warnings destroyed the unity of the squad, he knew she would never forgive herself.

CHAPTER

The next morning before school started, Jessica was standing in the front hall of Tarenton High, telling Melissa, Hope, Olivia, and Sean about her weird experience the previous evening. "It was uncanny," she told them. "I had just heard Patrick talking about horror movies when we were at the Pizza Palace, and then this happened. If I didn't know better, I'd think I was dreaming."

"Are you sure you weren't?" Sean asked innocently.

Jessica gave him a dirty look. "I thought my friends would be on my side, even if no one else is."

Sean beamed at her, flashing his perfect white teeth. "Oh, I'm on your side. Whatever that is. I just think you're out of your mind."

"With a vote of confidence like that, what

more could she ask?" said Melissa sarcastically.

"There certainly are a lot of weird things going on lately," said Olivia. She told the group how Madame Magda's prediction about her wearing a rose in her hair had come true.

Then Sean told the story of the psychic's appearance at the mall.

Melissa looked nervous. "I'm not sure I want to go to the game tonight after all, even if it is my chance to cheer. What if Tara is right?"

Hope hadn't said much so far. She had been too busy with her schoolwork and her music to pay much attention to the fuss over Tara and Madame Magda. But now, she realized, the problem was getting serious. "If Kate Harmon thinks Madame Magda's performance at the mall was a trick, then I'm sure she's right," she said.

Instead of calming everyone down, Hope's statement started a new babel of conversation.

"But what about the prediction she made to me?" Olivia protested.

"And what about my prowler?" asked Jessica.

"What prowler?"

The question was asked by Tara, who had joined the group unnoticed while Hope was talking. Under her new carmel-colored leather jacket, Tara was wearing a French-cut v-neck sweater. Even more eye-catching were her legs, encased in skin-tight beige leather slacks.

No one answered Tara's question. They were all too busy taking in her outfit. Tara seemed pleased by the attention. "I borrowed these pants from Diana," she told them. "She's lost weight since she bought them, so they're a little too baggy on her."

"You certainly don't have that problem," said Sean.

Tara decided to take the remark as a compliment, even if it hadn't been meant that way. Ever since she had been kicked out of practice, Tara's friends had hardly spoken to her, and she was willing to put up with a little sarcasm for the sake of being accepted. "So tell me about your prowler," she asked Jessica again.

Jessica repeated the story, and the others watched with interest as Tara's face drained of color.

"That's awful," she said, finally. "I mean, it's terrible that the dispatcher wouldn't believe you. What if you had been in real danger?"

"How do you know she wasn't?" Hope shot back.

Tara gasped. "I don't know. I was just assuming that. Surely, you don't think I know anything about this!"

"Of course not," Jessica put in, trying to make peace.

"I think you guys are all being unfair," Tara said, her eyes brimming with tears. "Just because I tried to warn you all about the game, for your own good, Coach Engborg is angry with me. And not one of you has stuck up for me."

"How can we defend you?" Olivia protested. "You never tried to come back to practice. You don't want to go to the game tonight. You're the one who deserted us!"

"I did not," Tara retorted. "But I can't force you to listen to my warning if you don't want to. Just wait and see. Tonight we'll find out whether or not Madame Magda's prediction is true."

With that, Tara tossed her long red hair over one shoulder and turned her back on the group.

"That sounded like another prediction," said Olivia as she watched Tara stalk down the hall toward her locker. "I admit, I'm starting to feel scared, but I have no intention of letting Tara bully me into missing a basketball game."

"I agree," said Jessica. "I'm a little nervous, too. But I'm definitely going."

"Me, too," said Sean.

Naturally, Hope agreed also. She was the only member of the squad who hadn't noticed anything strange over the last few days, and her logical mind demanded answers. "I don't care what you say," she told the others. "I was watching Tara's face when Jessica told her story about the mysterious prowler. I'm convinced she knows more than she's telling, and I intend to find out what it is."

Hope's vow sounded impressive, but the truth was she had no idea how she was going to live up to it. The Danville game was scheduled for eight o'clock that very evening. How could she possibly figure out what was going on before then?

Tara certainly wasn't about to volunteer any information. Hope tried to get her alone to talk to her several times that day, but wherever Tara was, Diana Tucker was right beside her. The two of them seemed to have become inseparable.

By the time the afternoon rolled around, Hope was resigned to the fact that she wasn't going to learn anything important at school. Fortunately, she had a last period study hall on her schedule that day, and juniors and seniors who had a free last period were permitted to leave school early. Usually, she didn't take advantage of this privilege. She preferred to use the time to study in the library or practice in the orchestra room, and anyway, most days she had cheerleading practice right after last period. Today, however, the extra time might make all the difference.

Using the public phone in the front hall, she called the office of H & T Movers. She was hoping to reach Tony Pell, who worked for Patrick most afternoons and weekends. Instead, Patrick answered and told her that Tony was out on a job and wouldn't be back for a few hours.

"That's too bad," Hope said, and she explained to Patrick why she wanted Tony. "I've got to get some answers, and the only place I can think of to find them is Madame Magda's house. I'm just determined to know what she's up to."

"In that case," said Patrick, "I'll be glad to help. This psychic powers stuff is ruining my love life. How can I kiss a girl when she's worrying about getting her aura wrinkled?"

Hope laughed. "Leave it to you to look at the

practical side of the issue! But won't Tara be furious if she finds out that you're trying to help me?"

"I have to take that chance," Patrick told her. "At first, I tried not to get involved, and that certainly didn't work. I just have to hope that once Tara comes to her senses, she'll realize I was just trying to help her."

Tony was driving one of the moving vans, and the other one was in the shop at the moment, so Patrick promised to come by the school on his cycle to pick up Hope.

"Maybe I'd better come out to the road to meet you," she suggested. "If Tara sees us together she might think we're up to something behind her back, and then she'll be more upset than ever."

"That's her problem," Patrick said decisively. "I don't want to upset her, but there's got to be some trust, or our relationship doesn't mean anything."

So fifteen minutes later, Patrick Henley pulled up in front of the main door of Tarenton High, and Hope ran out and jumped on the back of his cycle.

It didn't help. Tara didn't see them drive away. But others did, and by the time the last period of the day ended, word of Hope's "date" with Patrick had spread through the school, almost as if by magic. Three different people had told Tara the news by the time she got to her locker.

As for Patrick, he was elated at the prospect of

confronting Madame Magda. "That woman has really messed up Tara's head," he told Hope when they stopped at a red light on their way through the town. "I can't wait to give her a piece of my mind."

"Uh-oh," Hope muttered to herself. Patrick's cocky attitude made her uneasy. Sean had approached Madame Magda with the same attitude and now he was half convinced that her powers were genuine. She was really sorry that Tony hadn't been around the garage when she called. Tony was no professor when it came to schoolwork, but he had patience and street smarts, and Hope had learned to respect his intelligence.

When they got to Madame Magda's house, she had to talk Patrick out of marching up to the door right away. "There's no point in going in without a plan," Hope reminded him.

"I don't *need* a plan," Patrick contradicted her. "Not when I know I'm right."

Hope may have been half Patrick's size but she was his equal when it came to stubbornness. Soon the two of them were so involved in their argument that they didn't even notice when Madame's front door opened and a familiar figure appeared on the doorstep.

Holly Hudson, the leader of Tarenton High's Pompon Squad, noticed Hope and Patrick at once. "Hi, there!" she greeted them. "Don't tell me you've come to consult Madame M., too!"

Hope felt as if a lightbulb had been switched on inside her head. "Do you mean to say you've been here before?" she asked.

Holly nodded. "Of course. I've been seeing Madame M. ever since she arrived in town. At first, I was hoping she could predict the scores of the forthcoming basketball games, but Madame says she doesn't do predictions like that. She did tell me, though, that I had an aptitude for this psychic stuff. She said I have this aura that she can actually see. And you'll never guess what color it is!"

"Purple," said Patrick.

Holly's eyes opened wide in amazement.

"I think I'm psychic, too," Patrick told her, trying to suppress a grin.

"Gee, that's great," Holly exclaimed. "Anyway, I came today to find out about Madame M.'s prediction about tonight's game. She says she can't explain exactly what her vision meant, but anyway, Tara was in it. So if Tara doesn't go, nothing bad can happen."

Patrick's smile vanished. "That sounds like a threat to me. I'm going to give that woman a piece of my mind."

Hope grabbed Patrick's arm just in time to prevent him from stomping off in the direction of Madame Magda's doorstep. "Forget it," she advised. "Don't you see what this means?"

Patrick and Holly both looked blank.

"Holly has been talking to Madame Magda all along," Hope explained. "She told her all about the basketball team's forthcoming games. I bet she told her things about the cheerleaders, too. That's how she was able to make so many accurate predictions."

Holly nodded. She looked alarmed. "I didn't mean any harm, honest."

"We know you didn't," Hope and Patrick said in unison. Holly would never do anything deliberately mean. She was just too easily influenced. It was easy to imagine her pouring her heart out to Madame Magda and never stopping to think that everything she talked about was helping Madame Magda look good.

Hope checked her watch. "School's already out for the day," she told Patrick. "Forget about Madame Magda. She isn't worth it. There's just a few hours between now and the time we all have to meet for the trip to Danville. I think we ought to use the time to talk to the rest of the squad and explain to them that they have nothing to worry about."

Tara couldn't remember when she'd had such an awful day. Her problems had started that morning as soon as she heard Jessica tell the story of her mystery prowler. Contrary to what Hope seemed to think, she had no part in frightening Jessica. But she knew instantly who was responsible.

She caught up with Diana Tucker just before second period, as Diana was changing for her girls' basketball class.

"How could you do that?" she challenged her. "You said that no one was going to get hurt."

Diana nonchalantly ran a styling brush through her fine blonde hair. "So? Jessica didn't get hurt, did she?"

"She was really scared, though."

"Big deal." Diana shrugged sulkily. "If you recall, making everyone scared was the point of our little game."

Tara felt a hard knot of anxiety in her stomach. It was true that she and Diana had planned to use the old wolf suit to scare the cheerleaders into skipping the Danville game. "But we never said anything about going to people's houses," she reminded Diana. "We were going to stage our little scene in the parking lot tonight, when everyone is meeting to board the buses going to Danville."

"True. But I needed a dress rehearsal. And I figured Jessica Bennett was the easiest mark."

Diana smirked back at her image in the mirror. "It worked great, too. Even better than I would have expected. I fixed the wolf mask up a bit, and put some vaseline and stuff on the fur so it wouldn't look quite so ratty. It still wouldn't fool anybody for long, but in the dark, for just a second or two, I must have really been terrifying."

"People see what they expect to see," Diana added smugly. "If they want to be scared, then it's easy to oblige them."

"Well, I want out," Tara said. "This is getting out of hand. I say we call off our plan for this evening."

"Is that what you really want?" Diana taunted her. "And let your friends drive straight into danger?"

"Of course not. There's got to be another

way . . . ," Tara stuttered. She couldn't think of one, though.

Diana turned around, hands on hips, and glared at her. "We've already decided to do it this way, and it's too late to change now. You helped me steal the wolf suit from the storeroom and you're involved whether you like it or not. Besides, if you chicken out, don't expect me to protect you. I'll make sure that Coach Engborg knows this little stunt was your idea."

Tara knew that Diana was one person who was capable of carrying out her threats. So what now? For the rest of the day she sleepwalked from one class to the next, hoping for some miracle that would get her out of trouble. It was a gray, cloudy day, so with luck maybe a storm would blow up and force Tarenton and Danville to cancel the game. Maybe the whole Danville team would come down with the flu. Or maybe *she* could come down with the flu — then at least she would be safely at home, being nursed by her mother, and not have to know how the evening turned out until it was all over.

Realistically, though, there was no way she could stay away from the scene of the action. Hope already suspected her, and if anyone recognized the wolf suit tonight, she was the first person they'd expect to be wearing it. The only way to divert suspicion was to hang around with the group that was going to ride the Pompon Squad bus. That way she could make sure there were plenty of witnesses who could prove she had been minding her own business all evening long.

Even so, if Diana got caught and ratted on her, she could very well be kicked off the cheerleading squad for good.

Tara's head ached. How had she ever let herself get into such a mess? All she wanted to do was protect her friends. Why was it that every time she tried to do someone a good turn she ended up in deep trouble?

CHAPTER

By six o'clock that evening, the gray clouds that had hung over Tarenton all day had begun to descend. A chilly, damp mist had enveloped the town, and in some low-lying spots, like the high school parking lot, the fog was getting thicker by the minute.

Coach Engborg was standing near the cheerleaders' minibus, her arms folded in front of her as she surveyed the situation. There were very few things that made the coach anxious, but driving in bad weather was one of them. A bit tentatively, she walked to the other side of the parking lot, where the bus chartered by the Pompon Squad was waiting.

"I've seen a lot worse than this," the driver said, trying to reassure her. "Anyway, the team already left half an hour ago, so you can bet the game won't be canceled. Just keep your low beams on and be careful. You'll come through all right."

While she was talking with the bus driver, Coach Engborg noticed Tara Armstrong standing with the group waiting to board the bus and chatting with Carla Simpson and Andy Poletti, whose sister Angie had been a cheerleader last year.

"I'm surprised to see you here," the coach said, approaching Tara with a frown. "I thought your guru, or whoever she is, had ordered you to stay away."

Andy and Carla giggled. But Tara tried to look calm and unrepentant. "Madame Magda is not a guru," she said evenly. "And she didn't order me to do anything. I was just trying to warn all of you because she predicted trouble. And since no one would listen, I'm here to support my school, sink or swim."

Andy laughed again, but this time there was an undertone of doubt in his voice. "This fog is so thick you almost could swim in it," he observed. "Maybe Tara's psychic was right."

Coach Engborg tightened her lips. "I'll have none of that talk. The bus driver is a professional, and he says there's no problem. That's good enough for me."

"As for you, young lady," she added, turning to Tara, "I never thought you'd be the one to turn your back on the squad."

"But Coach, that isn't fair," Tara pleaded.

Tara looked so miserable that Coach Engborg couldn't stay angry with her. "I suggest that you come to see me in my office before homeroom

Monday morning. By then, this nonsense will be over, and we can discuss reinstating you on the squad."

"Thanks, Coach Engborg," said Tara none too enthusiastically. Silently, she wondered whether the coach's invitation would still be open on Monday morning. A lot could happen between now and then.

Back at the minibus, the rest of the squad was gathering.

Olivia, who showed up first, was surprised to see that David Duffy was already on hand, leaning against the door of the minibus, his camera bag under his arm.

"Don't tell me you've been assigned to cover tonight's game," she remarked sarcastically. "Why is it that the *Tarenton Lighter* never bothered to assign a full-time reporter to the varsity team until recently?"

"That was an oversight," he shot back. "But one I intend to correct."

Olivia was annoyed with Duffy for hanging around, but at the same time she couldn't help feeling flattered by all the attention he paid her. He could be insufferably self-centered. But he was also entertaining, not to mention attractive. Tonight he was wearing his double-breasted trench coat again, and looked more than ever like a private eye from an old movie.

"You know what this weather reminds me of?" she said aloud. "It reminds me of the final scene in the movie *Casablanca*. The one where they all meet at the airport. That was shot on a misty night, too."

Duffy scowled. "Can't we do a scene from some other film? As I recall, that one ends with Humphrey Bogart giving up Ingrid Bergman so she can leave Casablanca with her husband."

He leaned closer to Olivia, so close she could smell the faint, leathery odor of the after-shave cologne he liked to wear. "I'm not cut out for that role. Let Walt be the one to make the noble sacrifices."

"Let's not get too melodramatic," she warned.

Duffy grimaced. "Here I am pouring out my heart to you, and you accuse me of being too melodramatic."

"But Duffy! You pour out your heart to me all the time lately. What I'd really like is to be left alone for a change."

Duffy looked mildy offended. "Okay, okay. If you feel that way about it, I'll go over and talk to some of the kids who are riding in the Pompon Squad bus."

"Good idea."

Duffy carefully reshaped the brim of his battered Stetson so that it sat at a more rakish angle, then strolled away, his camera bag tucked under his arm. After two steps he turned and winked. "I know you're going to miss me desperately, but try to bear up under the strain. I'll be back in fifteen minutes."

Olivia sighed. "I should have known."

A few feet away, Hope was standing alone,

feeling slighted. She had expected everyone to be grateful when she told them about the results of her investigation of Madame Magda's sources of information. Instead, it seemed as if her efforts were almost resented.

"You sound just like Kate," Sean had told her when she phoned him earlier with the news. "I know what the two of you are saying is logical, but if you actually experienced some of these things you wouldn't be so sure you're right."

Olivia had said much the same thing.

And so had Peter.

Jessica's reaction was even stronger. She knew what she had seen — she was even surer now than she'd been at the time. "Boy, weird things are going on in Tarenton. I don't know exactly what's causing them, but you'll never convince me that anyone as harmless as Holly Hudson is behind all of this. She may be a little bit flakey, but she would never do anything to deliberately hurt anyone."

Hope and Patrick hadn't even been able to talk to Tara. When the two of them arrived at the Armstrong house shortly after leaving Madame Magda's, she had acted jealous and huffy. "It's bad enough that you left school last period to go off with Patrick on his motorcycle," she told Hope accusingly. "Now the two of you have the nerve to come to my house to tell me you think I'm crazy."

"No one said you were crazy!" Hope exclaimed, but it was obvious that there was no point in trying to continue the observation. She and Patrick both felt sure that Tara was just putting on an act, pretending jealousy to cover up her unhappiness about being off the squad for tonight's game. But what could they say to comfort her when she acted so touchy?

Patrick had been planning to take Tara to the game if she wanted to go. But for some reason he didn't understand her insisting on riding in the Pompon Squad bus, so he gave up in exasperation. "In that case," he told her, "I'm going to go back to the office. I still haven't finished doing my bills."

At that point, Hope had left the two of them arguing and walked home on her own.

By the time she got to the school parking lot, she was starting to think that maybe there was something weird in the air after all. Maybe the others were right and she was wrong. Everyone was certainly acting strangely. And even competent, confident Coach Engborg was nervous about the drive to Danville.

And for what? Sure, it was foggy. But people in the North Country took pride in their ability to cope with bad weather.

Bored with waiting around, Hope thought of the novel she was reading for English class that she had left in her locker. The cleaning crew was still at work in the main wing of the school and the lights were still on. Probably the front doors were still open.

Impulsively, she went around to the front of the building and tugged on the heavy brass handles. Two of the sets of double doors were locked, but the third set had been propped open with a wooden wedge.

Slipping inside, Hope crossed the front hall and strode purposefully toward the north wing hallway, where her locker was located. Light from the open doors of the classrooms spilled out into the darkened hallway. From the chemistry lab came the sound of a radio blaring rock music. Hope glanced inside and saw a janitor, singing along as he attacked the floor with a mop.

After that, she didn't worry as much about making noise. Confidently, she retrieved the paperback book from her locker and made her way back to the front hall.

She didn't start feeling nervous until she noticed that the block of wood which had been holding open the doors had been moved aside, and all three sets of doors were securely locked. One of the doors was a fire exit, so she could have gotten out if she were really desperate. But not without setting off the alarm.

"No way," said Hope aloud. Coach Engborg was already on edge. There was no sense trying her patience further before the trip had even begun.

Thinking over her options, Hope remembered that the back door of the school, leading directly to the locker rooms, would probably still be open. The team and the cheerleaders would be changing in the locker rooms at Danville High. But still, the team managers had to be able to get into the gym to pick up the uniforms and equipment.

The main staircase was completely dark. The cleaning crew must have finished their work on the lower level. Holding tightly to the bannister, she eased her way down the steps. It's really amazing how much people depend on their sight, she thought, as she explored the width of each step with her foot before committing herself. She climbed that staircase every school day, but in the darkness it seemed completely unfamiliar. She couldn't even remember how many stairs there were.

It was odd, too, how the old wooden bannister seemed to be vibrating almost as if someone else were hanging on to it. Abruptly she turned and peered into the shadowy stairwell. She couldn't be entirely sure, but she had the impression that a dark shape had ducked back around the corner to avoid being seen.

"Who's there?" she called out. "Is someone there?"

She had tried to sound confident and challenging. But her voice, echoing in the empty stairwell, sounded hollow and quavering.

Unfortunately, the lower level exit was at the opposite corner of the building. Considering which way to go, Hope decided to walk to her right, through the cafeteria, where two low-wattage light bulbs were burning. The cafeteria, usually so busy and cheerful, even after lunch when it served as a study hall, looked forbidding in the dim light. The tall stacks of plastic chairs cast long shadows. The steamtable trays had been removed, and the water standing in the catch basin underneath cast rippled shadows on the ceiling.

Turning down the long east hall, she tried to force herself to walk calmly but quietly. But her rubber-soled shoes had chosen this moment to start squeaking. No matter what she did, they made an irritating squeegee sound with almost every step she took.

The east hall was even darker than the cafeteria. For a long stretch in the middle of the hall there were no classrooms and no windows. Just a series of deep bays, lined with students' lockers.

Suddenly, she heard a noise coming from the last of the long bays. She whirled around. Something furry and oddly sticky brushed her hand. Then she saw a gaping mouth, with two rows of teeth the size of a shark's fangs and so white they seemed to glow in the dark.

This was no time for logic. Jerking her hand away, she sprinted for the rear exit.

She didn't slow down until she had burst into the cold outdoor air and crossed the parking lot to the place where the cheerleaders were gathered by the waiting minibus.

"I saw it," she told them, gasping for breath. "It was following me."

Coach Engborg took charge immediately. "Now calm down and tell me exactly what happened," she demanded.

As Hope told of being stalked through the deserted school, the coach's face was filled with alarm and concern. Then Hope began describing the creature itself . . . its hairy touch . . . its huge, gleaming teeth.

Coach Engborg rolled her eyes in disbelief. "Are you trying to tell me that this 'thing' wasn't a human being?"

"I don't think so," Hope admitted.

"I'm disappointed in you," the coach said. "I thought you were too sensible to give in to this hysteria."

"I'm not hysterical," Hope insisted.

But Coach Engborg cut her off. "The minibus is departing in exactly two minutes, and I expect anyone who considers him or herself still a member of the squad to be on board. Is that clear?"

The cheerleaders exchanged doubtful looks.

Finally, Hope spoke up. "I certainly don't intend to stay here in this creepy fog, so I guess you can count me in."

One by one, the others muttered agreement and took their seats in the minibus.

As Coach Engborg started the engine, Peter started to sing "Three Cheers for Tarenton High." One by one, the others joined in, with Sean's baritone contributing some off-key harmonizing.

No one said a word about being afraid, but Hope was still feeling a bit shaky. She was grateful when Jessica Bennett reached over and gave her hand a comforting squeeze.

CHAPTER

On board the Pompon Squad bus, Tara was having an attack of conscience.

She had been watching from a window seat as Hope came flying out the rear door of the school, looking utterly terrified. Then, minutes later, she saw the minibus turn on its headlights and drive out of the parking lot. Diana's disguise must be working even better than she claimed if she had managed to scare Hope Chang. As far as Tara was concerned, it was working a little bit too well. No matter how scared she was of being stuck with the blame, she couldn't sit by any longer and watch Diana terrorize the squad.

Abruptly, she jumped out of her seat and raced for the doors just as the driver was about to close them for the last time.

"Hey there, Red!" the driver shouted at her.

"Don't leave now or you'll miss the bus. I'm not waiting for you."

"That's okay," she shouted back over her shoulder. "I've changed my mind."

"Crazy kids," the driver muttered.

David Duffy was standing by the open trunk of his car, studying a map of the route to Danville. "Duffy!" Tara called out to him. "How'd you like to take a great picture?"

"Sure," he said amiably. "Is it newsworthy?"

"I don't know if it will make the front page of the *Lighter*," Tara answered. "But it will be news to some people."

Duffy fished into his camera bag and pulled out his 35-millimeter camera. "I've got fast film and a flash attachment," he said, "but we'll still have to be pretty close to get a good shot in this mist."

"I'll do my best," Tara assured him. "Just follow me."

Carefully circling the floodlit area of the parking lot nearest the school, Tara led Duffy around to the far side of the building and through the border of trees that lay between the school grounds and the county road. Just as she had thought, Diana Tucker's white Volkswagen was parked on the shoulder of the road.

Duffy looked at her questioningly. "What's this all about?" he asked. "I didn't see Diana around school."

"Just wait," Tara told her. "We'll duck down behind the car and surprise her when she shows up."

Not five minutes later, Tara spotted a dark silhouette coming their way from the direction of the school. "Here she comes," she whispered to Duffy. "Get ready to snap her picture."

Duffy silently counted to ten, then leaped from behind the car, snapping away. The first blaze of light from his automated flash attachment caught Diana looking absurdly guilty. Her face wore a ridiculous pop-eyed expression. One hand was instinctively raised to ward off the camera. And in the other arm she held the wolf's-head mask. She tried to run away, but she was still wearing the rest of the wolf's suit, and as she started back towards the trees, she managed to stumble over the tail.

"That's an outstanding outfit," Duffy told her cheerfully. "It really makes a statement. I think the tail is a bit formal, though."

Diana quickly reverted to her usual pouty expression. "You scared me," she said accusingly.

"Let me get this straight," Tara said. "It's okay for you to scare Hope and Jessica, but no one is supposed to scare you?"

"That wasn't me who scared Hope," Diana said, lying easily.

"Right," said Duffy sarcastically. "That must have been someone else in a wolf suit."

It dawned on Diana that this was one time when denying responsibility wasn't going to work. "Okay," she said, "it was me. But there's nothing you can do about it."

"That's what you think," Duffy told her. "I've got the evidence right here on film."

Diana glared defiantly at Tara. "If you let him use that I'll be sure to tell the coach that you were in on the plan to scare the cheerleaders out of going to the game from the beginning."

"Is that true?" Duffy asked Tara.

"I'm afraid so," she admitted. "I wanted to keep the squad from leaving for Danville for their own protection. But it didn't even work. They got scared all right, but the minibus left anyway."

Diana grinned wickedly. "Maybe the plan didn't work from your point of view. But it wasn't a total failure."

"What's that supposed to mean?" Tara asked.

"Just that when the squad gets to Danville they're in for a big surprise. Because they don't have their uniforms."

"You didn't!" Tara gasped. "You took them!"

"It was too easy to resist," Diana said. "Olivia and Melissa put the uniforms in the minibus after school. Then they hung the key to the minibus on a hook in the coach's office. I waited until they left and then took the uniforms out of the storage compartment and hung them back up in the girls' locker room. When Coach Engborg finds out they're missing she'll never believe that they were moved. I bet you anything she'll think Olivia and Melissa just forgot about them."

"You . . . you snake!" Duffy exploded. "Olivia was driving herself crazy all week long trying to put together a routine for this game. All those kids work so hard, and all you ever do is make trouble for them. What's wrong with you anyway?"

Diana's self-satisfied smirk faded. "Why should I feel sorry for them? They get all the attention. They're the big wheels around this school. I'm just trying to even the odds a little bit."

"I'll even the odds . . ." Duffy muttered.

Tara had never seen Duffy lose his cool so completely. She grabbed his arm. "Come on," she urged. "Let's not waste our time arguing with her. We still have time to get those uniforms and deliver them to Danville High. But if we want to get there in time, we'd better get going."

The rear doors of the school were already locked, so Duffy had to find the head custodian and persuade him to let them in to get the uniforms. Then they loaded the uniforms into Tara's Chevy, which had a larger trunk than Duffy's car. Tara insisted on driving.

"I thought you were the one who was so scared about making this trip," Duffy reminded her.

"Not anymore. It's strange, but now that I have something practical to do, I've almost forgotten about that stuff."

"Good," said Duffy, "and while you're in a practical mood you can figure out what you're going to say to Coach Engborg when we show up with the missing uniforms."

"Maybe I won't have to say anything," Tara suggested. "Not if you can study that map of yours and find us a shortcut."

"No way. Count me out," Duffy protested. "I'm not getting involved in this."

But it wasn't easy to say no to Tara once she had made up her mind. Duffy consulted his map and found a route that ran through the river valley and was mostly clear of fog. When they reached Danville High the players and the Pompon Squad had arrived, but the minibus was nowhere in sight.

"Great," exulted Tara. "We're here first. Now when the minibus gets here, you insist on posing everyone for a group portrait in front of the building."

"This will *never* work," Duffy predicted. But when the minibus arrived, he followed Tara's instructions. "Step right this way, people," he told the startled cheerleaders. "I need a shot for the *Lighter*."

"Now?" Coach Engborg asked in amazement. "But the kids don't even have their uniforms on. . . ."

And they won't either, unless they cooperate, Duffy thought as he ushered everyone to the steps of the school and carefully posed them with their backs to the minibus. "Never mind," he said aloud. "I need this for a deadline. Now say 'cheers.' "

While he fussed over his camera, pretending to take his time setting the exposure and shutter speed, Tara was running frantically back and forth between the Chevy and the minibus, replacing the uniforms in the minibus's cargo locker. Normally, no one Duffy knew was more careful to avoid ordinary physical labor than Tara, and the sight of her staggering under an armload of sweaters, pompons, and miscellaneous gear, while her long legs skittered at top speed, was hilarious. It was all he could do to keep a straight face.

Even so, by the time he had taken two pictures and was rearranging the squad for a third group pose, they were starting to get suspicious.

"We like to cooperate with the press, David," said Coach Engborg, "but perhaps we could do this later. There *is* a game tonight, last I heard."

Olivia was more direct. "I don't know what you're up to David Duffy. But we don't have all night to humor you."

"Just one more shot," he begged.

"Forget it, old man," said Sean.

Fortunately, Tara had just safely stowed away the last of the uniforms and gear. Unfortunately, she had decided to press her luck by dumping the wolf's suit into the cargo locker as well. It didn't really belong there. But she had forced Diana to give the suit back, and now she was desperate to get the incriminating costume out of the trunk of her car.

Coach Engborg turned around and caught sight of her just as she was hustling over to the minibus for the last time, carrying the rolled-up costume and mask under one arm.

"Why, Tara! What a nice idea!" said the coach, in a voice so sweet it could have been served on waffles.

"N-Nice?" stammered Tara guiltily.

"Why, yes," continued Coach Engborg. "Since you aren't cheering with us tonight, I see you've decided to make a contribution to the Pompon Squad by wearing that old mascot's suit. Of course, it's a bit ratty looking. But I know you won't mind sacrificing your vanity for the sake of a few good laughs."

"Mind? Uh, no. Of course not."

Duffy had to suck in his cheeks to keep from howling with laughter. No one had ever suggested before that Tara Armstrong, glamorous, image-conscious Tara, would willingly sacrifice her vanity for a good cause, much less play the clown in front of a packed auditorium. Tara looked utterly horrified.

But Hope and Jessica were already studying the wolf's-head mask with looks of appalled recognition. It was going to be tough enough getting them to forgive her without having to tell her whole story on the spot, in front of Coach Engborg.

"Right," said Tara, gritting her teeth. "Anything for a joke."

CHAPTER

14

On their way into the visitors' area of the girls' locker room, Melissa and Olivia peered into the Danville High gym and gasped. Every seat in the stands was taken, and an enormous banner stretched across the opposite wall of the gym proclaimed:

GO, RED DEVILS! WALLOP THE WOLVES!

It was obvious that the Danville crowd, at least, was taking the exhibition game very seriously.

"I don't get it," said Olivia, "I thought this game didn't count toward the conference standings. It's just an extra."

"Maybe to you Tarenton kids," said the Danville girl who was showing them to their lockers, "but that's not the way we see it. Danville used to be a power in basketball. We were even state champs one year. Then we lost enrollment and were demoted to the 'B' league. But we've merged with another school now, and we're on the way back up."

"And you're planning to prove yourself by demolishing Tarenton High," Melissa guessed.

"Right!" said the girl. "You've got it!"

"Don't celebrate yet," Olivia warned her. "We're taking this game seriously, too."

But were they?

So far, she couldn't exactly say that the cheerleaders were. True, she'd worked out an exciting new routine with Ms. Frazier's help, but the squad had spent just one practice working on it. No one had seemed very worried about this at the time, Coach Engborg included, and Olivia realized now that they'd all been thinking of the Danville game as a chance to work on the squad's new material.

Another problem was that Tara Armstrong, normally the squad's spark plug, wasn't even going to be cheering tonight. Melissa was well prepared to take her place, as far as knowing the routines went. But cheering in front of a crowd, especially at an away game, was completely different from cheering in practice.

Melissa, as if reading Olivia's mind, was suddenly looking very pale. "I hate to say this," she confessed, "but I feel a serious attack of stage fright coming on."

"You'll do great," Olivia tried to reassure her. "After all, you've danced in front of audiences

129

before. This is no different. In fact, it'll be easier. Once you get caught up in the spirit of cheering, it isn't like performing at all."

"I hope you're right," Melissa said, none too confidently.

As for Jessica and Hope, they had latched on to Tara, determined to get the whole story of the wolf's suit. "That's the mask my prowler was wearing," Jessica said accusingly.

"It's what I saw, too," Hope concurred. "You have some heavy explaining to do, Tara."

Tara wasn't looking forward to telling her story, and she was relieved when Olivia called off Jessica and Hope. "If we don't get out on that floor right away, we'll miss the start of the game," she warned them. "There'll be plenty of time for straightening this out later."

When they did bound into the gym a few minutes later, they felt like unarmed gladiators being thrown into the arena with a pack of lions. The Danville fans had had plenty of time to warm up, and they were screaming their heads off.

"Ouch," said Olivia, "play hasn't even started yet. Talk about a tough crowd."

On the floor, the Danville cheerleaders were shouting:

"Our team is re-e-e-e-d hot!
Their team is all shot!"

"Talk about old cheers," Hope sniffed. "That one belongs to ancient history."

Even so, the look of the Danville squad more than made up for their stodgy repertoire of cheers. As Coach Engborg had said, the squad was coed; it was far from old-fashioned. The eight cheerleaders ranged in height from a pair of near six-footers to two petite girls barely five feet tall. Every one of them was striking-looking, as were their black and red uniforms.

Worst of all, they were good.

The Danville cheerleaders still did all the tricky, possibly dangerous, moves that the Tarenton squad had removed from their routines for safety reasons. They even did fancy vaults from a small portable trampoline.

"Let's put some extra oomph in our jumps tonight," Olivia told the others, "or we're going to look like losers in comparison to the Danville squad."

Following her own advice, she strutted out in front of the visitors' section and called out the first Tarenton cheer:

"Shout it far,
Shout it loud,
We are here,
We are proud."

Seconds later the opening whistle blew and the two teams began to scramble. On the Wolves' side, their tallest player, P. J. Thompson, was the only one who was really in the game. Everyone else was having trouble making rebounds and even more trouble passing and shooting when they managed to get their hands on the ball. They looked like a supporting cast of zombies, just going through the motions.

Desperate to wake up the Tarenton side, Olivia got Sean to sit her up on his shoulders so she could lead the call for defense.

"DEE-fense, DEE-fense," she yelled into the megaphone.

In the first row of the cheering section, David Duffy had forgotten that as a sportswriter he was supposed to be neutral. He had put down his notepad and pencil and was cheering along with the rest of the Tarenton section.

And sitting right beside him, cheering along with the rest was . . . Walt Manners.

Olivia was so startled by the sight of Walt that she almost lost her balance and pitched forward off Sean's shoulders. Lately, Walt and Duffy had been so allergic to each other's presence that they could barely stand to be in the same room together. Now, here they were, sitting side by side in the visitors' section.

For that matter, what was Walt doing at the game at all?

Olivia was happy to see him. She'd really been upset over Walt's "let's-go-steady-or-nothing" attitude. But now that he was here, she felt a surge of panic. That meant later this evening, they'd probably both ask her out for a post-game snack, and she'd have to decide which one to go with. And more likely than not, there would be some unpleasant repercussions from the one who lost out.

132

This was just the sort of situation that the "new Olivia" should have enjoyed. Some girls did, didn't they? Keeping two guys on a string, making them wonder which one you *really* liked, was supposed to be fun, wasn't it? But even though she tried to force herself to feel enthusiasm, Olivia dreaded being put on the spot. The more she tried to decide between Walt and Duffy, the more she felt that she liked both of them. If only she could split herself into two people, then she would never have to choose!

Olivia was so distracted, that for a minute or so she hardly noticed that Sean was tugging at her knee. "I don't mind holding you on my shoulders," he said through clenched teeth. "But not if you're just going to bob around up there like a sack of potatoes."

"Sorry," she said quickly, "then let me down."

None too graciously, Sean helped her with her dismount, and went off to do a three-person stunt with Peter and Hope.

"You look almost as scared as I feel," Melissa commented as Olivia took her place beside the alternate.

"I am," she confessed. "Only you're nervous about cheering, which is normal. I'm nervous because I wish the game would never end."

Why, she wondered, did she find life so much more scary than performing in public? Dating and relationships were supposed to be fun. But sometimes Olivia felt that for her, the priorities were reversed. At least in school and when she was cheerleading, she felt that she knew what was expected of her and could enjoy meeting the challenges that came up. When it came to emotions, it seemed there were no rules. None that were clearly spelled out, anyway.

A loud roar from the home team fans jolted Olivia from her reverie. She glanced at the scoreboard and saw that Danville had just widened its lead by twelve points. The Wolves were headed for disaster.

Then, as if on cue, the Danville mascot made its first appearance. The "Red Devil" was a kid in a silly-looking devil suit that looked like a Halloween reject. The suit itself was clearly just an ordinary set of tights and a leotard. The long tail was made of foam rubber and, bobbing behind the devil as he ran down the side of the court, it looked like an over-long cat's tail.

"Oh *please*," groaned Jessica as the Danville crowd welcomed its mascot with much cheering and stamping of feet.

"I guess that's the devil that Tara was in such a tizzy about," Peter said, laughing. "Not much to be afraid of, is it?"

Jessica made a quick survey of the gym with her eyes. "By the way," she put in, "where is Tara? I got the impression that Coach Engborg was more or less ordering her to make an appearance as the Tarenton High wolf. You don't suppose she's chickened out?"

"Nah, she'll show up," predicted Peter. "She can't afford to be in even more trouble with the coach. I'm sure she was just waiting for the Danville mascot to show up."

But in the girls' locker room, Tara was still struggling frantically with the zipper of the wolf's suit. Normally, she was agile enough to deal with a zipper that ran all the way up the back of an outfit, but this one was old and cumbersome. And worse yet, the suit itself was too tight.

Holding the back of the suit closed with one hand, she reached over her head with the other and pulled the tab closed with a determined jerk. The first two times she tried this maneuver, the zipper caught in the material of her sweater, leaving her hopping around in circles, frustrated and angry over the damage to one of her best outfits.

Finally, she gave up, climbed out of the suit, and changed her street clothes for an old Danville team T-shirt and a pair of red running shorts that she found hanging in an open locker. Without her bulky clothes, her awkward struggle with the wolf-suit zipper had better success. But the results were not exactly attractive. The suit was still uncomfortably snug.

Studying her appearance in the full-length mirror, Tara winced. Wolves were supposed to be lean and rangy. But she looked more like a roly-poly teddy bear!

Sean Dubrow, she remembered, had worn this old suit earlier in the year, for a school assembly. How, with his broad chest, had he ever fit into it?

Tara sighed. Knowing how vain Diana was, Tara guessed she had probably altered the suit to fit her own slender figure. Or else, she had washed the thing in the washing machine, causing it to shrink. Either way, there was nothing that could be done about the problem now.

Tara realized that she had two choices: She could spend the rest of the game in the locker room and then have one more broken commitment to explain to Coach Engborg. Or she could swallow her own vanity and go out on that floor looking like a cross between the abominable snowman and an overstuffed couch.

Thinking over the alternatives, Tara was torn. She might not be as self-conscious about her appearance as Diana. But if not, she came in a close second. The thought of looking ugly and clumsy in front of so many screaming fans filled her with dread.

On the other hand, she half suspected that Coach Engborg had not been fooled by Duffy's little distracting maneuver with the camera. The coach was pretty sharp, and she often knew more about what was going on behind her back than most of the kids on the squad suspected. But she had seemed willing to give Tara the benefit of the doubt, which was more than could be said for her fellow cheerleaders. They were pretty down on her for the way she had been acting, and Hope and Jessica especially weren't going to be too happy when they realized that Tara might have been able to stop Diana from scaring them, if only she hadn't been so scared about getting blamed.

"Oh well," she said aloud to her image in the mirror, "if you keep your mask on for the whole game, no one will ever have to know who you are. At least, no one but the other members of the squad."

Somewhat consoled by the thought, Tara donned the wolf's-head mask and, very cautiously, opened the door to the locker room and made her way along the passageway under the bleachers to courtside.

She had been half hoping that her arrival would go unnoticed. But, of course, that was impossible. How could anyone fail to notice? What's more, the Tarenton squad, eager for any excuse to whip up enthusiasm, made the most of Tara's entrance. While Olivia called for the "Growl, Wolves, Growl" cheer, Peter grabbed the mascot's hand and started skipping down the sidelines with her.

"Go easy," she begged him frantically.

"Wha'd you say?" shouted Peter. "I can't hear you."

Great! She could hardly move, hardly breathe, and hardly see. And for good measure, no one could hear her, either.

Trying desperately to remember the kind of cute maneuvers she'd seen costumed mascots do at other games, Tara sauntered up and down in front of the Tarenton bench, waved to the crowd, and then made a cautious foray in the direction of the home cheering section. The Red Devil was standing on the home team bench, facing the crowd, his ridiculous tail bouncing behind him.

That tail was just too good a target to overlook. Tara innocently sidled up to within a few feet of Danville territory, then lunged past the bench and gave the Danville mascot's tail a playful tweak. He turned around, waving his hands in mock outrage; but before he could retaliate, Tara had slipped back to the visitors' bench, where she stood between the Tarenton High coach and one of the referees.

Obviously the Danville Devil was going to try to think of a way to get back at her, but for the time being at least, she was safe.

On the court, the momentum of the action seemed to be shifting. The Tarenton five had figured out that they were in a real contest and were starting to come to life. They had just scored six points in a row, and the Danville team was starting to look discouraged.

To pep them up, the Danville cheerleaders started the team cheer:

> "Terry, Terry, he's our man,
> If he can't do it, Roger can . . .
> Roger, Roger, he's our man,
> If he can't do it, Jake can . . ."

The cheer was old hat, but the Danville squad had great moves, and Tara stopped to watch them, peering out through the gaps between the wolf mask's papier-mâché fangs.

"Jake, Jake he's our man," the cheer went on, "if he can't do it, Slick can."

Slick!

The name hit her like a wet dishrag in the face. Wasn't that the word Madame Magda had used? "I see something slick," she had said. Tara had assumed that meant a slick highway, a slippery spot in the road. But Madame Magda had never said that in so many words.

"Did they say Slick?" she all but shouted in the ear of the off-duty referee.

"Huh?" said the ref, not hearing her. But as she wildly gesticulated in the direction of the player wearing number eight for Danville, he got the message. "Slick Stevens," he said approvingly. "He just transferred here from out of state. He's very heavily recruited by the college scouts, too."

So that was it. Not only was this kid nicknamed Slick, he was a ringer, too.

Tara craned her neck to get a better look at the Tarenton team's chief competition. But just as she bent forward, she noticed a funny look on the referee's face and realized that he had just seen someone sneaking up behind her.

She jumped aside, just in time to prevent the Danville mascot from getting a good grip on her tail.

At that moment, the buzzer rang, announcing the end of the half, and the players began surging toward her, on their way to the locker rooms. Tara quickly slipped between two sweaty, panting players and scampered out onto the floor, daring the Danville mascot to catch her. He looked pretty slow, and she forgot for a moment that she wasn't exactly a speedball herself, wearing that tight, cumbersome suit.

Unfortunately, she soon discovered another of the problems her outfit posed. With her mask on, she could only see straight ahead, so there was no way to keep an eye on her pursuer without actually running backwards.

She was backpedaling across the floor, trying to figure out a way to escape, when she heard a burst of alarm from behind her. Obviously, it was a diversionary tactic, so she paid no attention. . . .

Ooomph!

The next thing she knew she was sprawled flat on her back. Luckily, the thing she had tripped over happened to be the Danville cheerleaders' minitrampoline, so she wasn't hurt. In fact, most of the crowd thought her tumble was intentional and were cheering enthusiastically.

Unluckily, her wolf's mask had not stopped when she did. As it went flying across the trampoline and landed on the floor, the pins holding Tara's hair in place were knocked loose, and her long red hair cascaded around her shoulders.

So much for anonymity! As she lay there on her back trying to catch her breath, one of the first faces she saw up in the stands was that of Patrick Henley, laughing uproariously.

But worst of all, as she fell, she had heard a horrible ripping sound, so loud that she was sure it must have been audible all the way up in the top row of the bleachers.

Tentatively, she felt behind her and confirmed her worst fears. The seat of the wolf's suit had split right up the middle. If she could, she would have been happy to just lie there on the trampoline for the rest of the game. Anything but to have to face the humiliation in store for her. But the Danville squad was waiting to use the trampoline, so there was nothing to do but get up.

As she did, the crowd noticed her red gym shorts peeking through the back of her torn costume and exploded all over again in a melee of cheers, whistles, and catcalls, while the Danville mascot pratically fell over his own feet in glee.

"This is awful. This is the most humiliating moment of my life!" she sputtered, as she made her way to the sidelines.

But Peter Rayman was grinning broadly. "Nonsense, you're a natural clown," he told her.

"That's right," said Sean, echoing the doubtful compliment. "Besides, look at it this way. You're probably the only wolf who ever drew wolf whistles."

"I guess you think that's clever," she snarled.

"You might as well be a good sport," Olivia pointed out. "As it is, most of the kids think you did it on purpose. So what do you have to lose?"

The Danville cheerleaders had finished their demonstration. Coach Engborg turned on the jitterbug music for Tarenton's halftime routine, and the squad ran out onto the floor.

Though she was still nursing her hurt pride, Tara had to admit that her squad-mates looked wonderful. Olivia had come up with some original choreography, and everyone was performing flawlessly. Melissa, who had made some mistakes out of nervousness earlier in the evening, had really come into her own, and she and Sean were performing a dazzling series of lifts interspersed with exuberant dance steps. Even the Danville fans, who had seemed downright hostile earlier, were caught up in the spirit, clapping along in time to the music.

The reception was so warm that when the tape ended, Coach Engborg quickly fast forwarded to the next track so that the squad could do an encore. Tara looked longingly at the cheerleaders on the floor. They were having so much fun, she would have loved to be out there with them — even in her embarrassing costume.

"So go ahead, go," Coach Engborg said, reading her mind. "You earned it."

Happily, Tara ran down the court, grabbed the hand of the Danville mascot, and dragged him out on the floor. "Come on," she shouted ecstatically. "Let's boogie!"

CHAPTER

15

"If that was a jinx game, I'd like to have a few more of them," Hope commented as she jogged into the locker room fifteen minutes after the final buzzer sounded.

No one put up an argument. After a bad beginning, the game had turned out to be almost perfect, and not just because Tarenton had rallied in the final quarter to win by three points. The jitterbug halftime routine had broken the ice, and after that the mood in the gym had been up-beat and basically friendly. The Danville fans were thrilled that their team could hold its own against a higher-rated school. And thanks to Tara and the Danville mascot, whose name turned out to be Howie Lawson, the two cheering squads had been able to meet and exchange tips for a few minutes after the game.

In one corner of the locker room, Jessica and

Hope were huddled with Tara, their anger forgotten, getting a rundown on Tara's attempts to keep them away from the game.

"I meant well, honest," Tara assured them. "I guess I just got carried away."

"At least there's one consolation," Jessica said. "Dreadful Diana won't get away with her troublemaking this time. She'll be out of school for good."

"I wouldn't be too sure about that," Hope said. "After all, what can we prove? She'll just say that she never meant to scare us; it was all a joke. And if we insist on making a big deal of it, we'll look like poor sports."

"I guess you're right," Jessica agreed reluctantly. "But I sure wish we could think of a way to pay back our Madame M. She could cause real trouble by making up horrible predictions like that. But I suppose it doesn't do any good to try to tell people."

Hope laughed. "It sure doesn't. I certainly learned that lesson."

Olivia was in a good mood as she changed from her uniform into her gray pleated slacks and rose-colored knit cowl top. It was good to see that the squad was unified again. She was so relaxed that she had almost forgotten about the Duffy vs. Walt problem.

Then she left the locker room and found Walt waiting just outside. "Hi," he said beaming. "Surprised to see me here tonight?"

"I guess I am," Olivia admitted. "I thought you couldn't stand to be within fifty feet of Duffy, and there you were sitting next to him, like an old buddy. What's up?"

"Oh, I guess I just had a change of heart. I realized that my being jealous was driving you away, and if I wasn't careful Duffy would win by default."

Olivia felt relieved. "I'm glad you saw that."

Walt adjusted his glasses, then straightened up and clapped his hands together. "Great. We solved that problem. Now let's get going. I've got plans for us. I figure we can get a burger with the rest of the gang. Then we can drop in at my place — did I tell you my aunt has fixed it so I have my own separate living space? Manners' manor, so to speak — to watch some old movies on the VCR. And tomorrow, we can drive up to Kearny Mountain . . ."

"Hey, wait a second," Olivia said, interrupting him. "Aren't you forgetting something?"

Walt turned his earnest, moon-faced look on her. "Gee, I don't think so. I even made reservations at that great lunch place up there."

"Yeah, but you did forget something," she insisted. "You forgot to ask me if I want to do these things with you. I mean, you can't just take it for granted. What if I had something else planned?"

Walt was the picture of injured innocence. "Do you?"

Actually, Olivia didn't, though it seemed like

quite a comedown to admit it now. "That isn't the point," she said. "It's the principle of the thing."

"Aw, come on," Walt pleaded. "I made friends with David Duffy. Isn't that enough to prove my good intentions for the time being?"

"Okay," she conceded. "Let's go out tonight. But we'll put all these other plans on hold for the time being. It isn't that I don't care for you. I do. But I think I need a chance to try my own wings, to be independent. And I can't do that if I'm spending practically all my time with one person."

Walt accepted this much better than Olivia would have expected. "I can live with that," he said seriously. "As long as the same rule applies to David Duffy."

"For now, it does," Olivia told him. "That's all I can tell you. I can't make any promises about the future."

Walt didn't look too pleased about that, but he nodded. "Fair enough, I guess."

Walt put his arm around her and they walked off toward his jeep.

"Tell me one thing," Olivia teased him, "how did you and Duffy ever end up sitting together at the game? That really threw me for a loop."

"Oh, I guess Duffy's not such a bad guy. That is, if you don't count the fact that he's a smart aleck and an egotist and trying to move in on my girl, to boot."

Olivia started to pull away, but Walt just laughed. "That part was supposed to be a joke.

Sort of. Anyway, Duffy and I are collaborating on a project. You'll find out all about it tomorrow evening, when Duffy's *3-D Radio Hour* is broadcast."

"A project? What is it?" The idea of Walt and Duffy on the radio together made Olivia extremely uneasy. She remembered all too well how Duffy had used his teen talk show to broadcast his own feelings about her when she broke up with him to go out with Walt.

Walt read her mind and gave her shoulder a comforting squeeze. "Don't worry," he said, "the project doesn't have anything to do with you. Well, maybe a little. But mostly not. It does affect the cheerleaders, though. But that's absolutely all I can tell you. You'll find out the rest tomorrow night."

Sean was in on Walt and Duffy's surprise, too, and by Saturday afternoon he had contacted all the cheerleaders to invite them to an informal party at his house that evening. "Be sure to come because we have a surprise for you," he promised.

Sean loved parties, but he wasn't known for giving them, so everyone was dying with curiosity to know what was going on. Olivia had been teasing Walt for hints, without success, and when she got to the Dubrow house that evening she immediately cornered Kate Harmon in the kitchen and tried to pump her for information.

"I don't know any more than you do," Kate told her. "Sean told me he wants me to be as surprised as anyone else."

147

Olivia looked around the kitchen. Not only had Sean's father bought a new refrigerator, but he had a brand-new range and microwave as well. "You don't suppose this has something to do with Mr. Dubrow remodeling the kitchen because he's getting married?" she asked.

Kate shrugged. "I don't think so. What would that have to do with Duffy and Walt?"

Besides the cheerleaders, including Melissa, Sean had invited Walt and Patrick and Hope's friend Tony Pell and Holly Hudson and a half dozen or so members of the Pompon Squad. He had even gone to the trouble of ordering an eight-foot-long hero from a deli that specialized in making giant sandwiches for parties. Sean's father had a great collection of old records, some of them going back to the fifties. Peter and Tony started going through the shelves, and before long they had found the old Rolling Stones records, an original Elvis Presley LP, and even a Buddy Holly record.

"This is fantastic," said Patrick. "I never realized your dad had this stuff. Some of these are real collector's items."

"Don't tell my old man that," Sean warned. "He thinks this is still new music. If he finds out these records are worth something, he won't want to let me play them."

Everyone wanted to dance, but they were just getting going when Sean turned the stereo off and signaled for silence. "You're probably wondering why I called you all together," he announced.

Patrick groaned. "That line is stale. You'll have to come up with something better than that to justify ordering me to shut off Elvis."

"I think I can manage that," he said. "I asked all you kids to come over because David Duffy is broadcasting a special edition of his radio show tonight. Walt and I helped him out on this one, so we wanted all of you to be here to listen to it."

Everyone looked at Walt, whose less than friendly feelings toward Duffy were well known.

Sean turned on the radio just in time to hear Duffy's familiar voice:

"Hi there, this is David Douglas Duffy, better known as 3-D, bringing you a special edition of *Teen Talk*. We're on at a different time tonight because we were able to arrange a live interview with a special guest, Madame Magda Halevy, Tarenton's own resident psychic. . . ."

Hope looked shocked. "I don't get it. No one was more down on Madame Magda than Duffy."

But no one could have told this from the interview that was coming over the radio. Madame obviously thought Duffy was a friend, and he was having no trouble getting her to reminisce about her great success in solving crimes and finding lost property.

"Vell, now I am looking forward to helping your police force here in Tarenton," Madame continued. "And of course, I will be available for consultations."

"At a price?" asked Duffy, scarcely masking the sarcasm in this voice.

"Oh, vell, I take donations, yes," Madame admitted modestly.

At that point, Duffy suddenly homed in. "Isn't it true, Madame, that you've been giving quite a lot of advice to certain students from our high school here in town?"

"I suppose so."

"For example, you told one young man that you saw the subject of marriage in his future."

The tape cut to an interview between Sean and Duffy:

". . . So when Madame Magda said that thing about marriage," Sean explained, "I thought that was really uncanny. Because I had just seen my dad in the appliance department with a woman he's been dating. So I had been talking to my friends about the possibility that there was a wedding in his future."

"Truly a remarkable prediction," intoned Duffy.

"My visions, zey tell me zeese tings," put in Madame, her accent more false-sounding than ever.

"But perhaps you had another source of information as well," Duffy added. "Let's listen to this interview, taped yesterday afternoon."

"My name is Walt Manners and I work at Carey Cycle in the mall. I happened to be working that afternoon and I saw Sean, Jessica, and Kate sitting in the cafe area. I also saw who was sitting at the table just behind them — Madame Magda. She was wearing a scarf and a coat with the collar turned up, so Sean and his friends wouldn't have noticed her. But I'm pretty sure she heard everything Sean was saying."

As Walt's voice faded out, Madame Magda came on the air, sputtering in indignation, her phony accent completely forgotten. "That's the most ridiculous charge I ever heard! I wasn't there. And if I was, so what?"

"Leaving that case," Duffy continued, his voice expressionless, "let's discuss another incident — a certain prediction you made concerning the Tarenton High basketball game last night. . . ."

"This is outrageous!" Madame Magda cried. "You have no right to investigate me. I won't stand for it!"

"That's too bad," Duffy countered, "I was thinking of making this a regular feature. I thought I could review your predictions every week. In fact, I already have a few of your former clients on the phone right now."

"I don't have to put up with this — this talking back, young man!" Madame retorted. She was so upset by now that it was obvious that she had good reason not to want to hear from people who had consulted her in the past. "I thought this was a straightforward interview. You never told me you were going to take phone calls."

"I guess I just figured you'd foresee it in one of your visions," Duffy said smoothly. "And now for our first caller, who's phoned into the station all the way from Detroit."

"Oh no you don't!"

There was a loud click, as someone in the studio slammed down a telephone receiver, then

151

a confused shuffling sound. Duffy calmly announced that Madame Magda was preparing to leave. But before departing for good, Madame Magda let loose her parting shot: "I've had it with you and all you impertinent Tarenton High kids! I'm going somewhere where I'll be appreciated!"

Hope clapped her hands. "I've got to hand it to Duffy. He did what I couldn't manage."

"Don't look at it that way," Walt told her. "It was you who got all of us thinking. That's when we started talking to each other about this."

Patrick Henley was laughing so hard he could barely sit upright. "That Duffy!" he howled. "It takes one to know one."

A few of the others looked at him in confusion. "What do you mean by that?" Tara asked.

"I think I know," Olivia put in. "There was no former client from out of town on the phone. Right?"

"Right," said Walt with admiration. "Duffy was just bluffing. He figured Madame Magda wouldn't be too happy to hear from people she had advised in the past. So he decided to take a chance, and he was right."

Olivia was glad Duffy's plan had worked, but she wasn't sure how she felt about him and Walt becoming friends. When the two of them were wildly jealous, she had felt torn between them. As much as she hated to admit it, though, the situation had been exciting. However miserable she had felt a lot of the time, she had also felt important.

Now, she wasn't sure what the future held. It was one thing to keep both Walt and Duffy on a string when they weren't speaking to each other. If they were buddies, that would be impossible. She might soon have to choose . . . one or the other, or . . . neither.

One thing she was more certain of than ever, she wasn't the same girl that Walt had gotten to know last year. As a junior, she would have been terrified at the thought of having the responsibility of being captain through some of the troubles the cheerleaders had faced so far this year. But so far, the squad had faced every challenge and had come through with flying colors. One thing she had learned was that she didn't have to solve every problem that came up singlehandedly. Leadership could sometimes be as simple as trusting others to pull together for the good of the squad.

"There's one prediction about the future that I don't mind making," she told the rest of the squad as they gathered around Sean's stereo. "You guys are the best bunch of friends I'll ever have."

Sean had turned off the radio and put on some of the old records Patrick had picked out, and a few at a time, couples began to dance.

Hope and Tony Pell were among the first couples to take the floor. Petite Hope, the A student with the logical but sometimes naive mind, seemed an unlikely match for "tough Tony," the motorcycle mechanic.

Watching them, it occurred to Jessica that Peter must have had some bad times when he and Hope broke up. Her experience in breaking up with Patrick had taught her how difficult it could be, even when it was your idea in the first place. Having to go through that with another member of the squad must be even worse. No wonder Peter was scared of getting involved again! Especially with another cheerleader!

For the last few days, she had been a little bit angry with Peter for being such an emotional ice cube. Now she was in a more understanding mood. Since the two of them were destined to be together so much, it made sense for them to get to know each other better — as friends, if not as two people in love.

A bit hesitantly, she crossed the room to where Peter was sitting. "How about saving the next fast dance for me?" she asked lightheartedly. "We could work on some new steps."

"I'd like that," said Peter.

For Tara, there were no regrets.

She was in Patrick's arms again, and more sure than ever that that was where she wanted to be.

"For a while there, I was afraid that two-bit psychic was going to do what no rival could," Patrick said, holding Tara close and gazing down into her eyes. "Break us up, I mean."

"If you even thought of it, then I'm glad she's

leaving Tarenton for good." Tara nestled happily against Patrick's shoulder as they began to dance together to the beat of one of his favorite old Presley numbers, "True Love."

The moment was perfect, her love was certainly true, but as Tara tried to lose herself in the pulsating slow chords of the music she couldn't help wondering . . .

Had Duffy and the others been too quick to dismiss Madame Magda as a complete fraud? True, she had tricked them. But there were things she had said that neither Walt nor Sean, nor anyone else for that matter, had explained. What about her prediction that Olivia would soon be wearing a flower in her hair? How could anyone have known about that in advance? And what about her episode on the gym floor during the Danville halftime — hadn't there been a crash of sorts, even if not the serious accident she had been expecting?

Tara would never again put her entire faith in anyone who claimed to have psychic powers. For one thing, knowing what the future held — or at least thinking that she knew — had only gotten her into trouble.

Still, the romantic in her clung to the notion that it might be possible to foresee the future after all. She'd learned the price of being gullible. But she didn't want to lose her faith in the power of imagination and dreams, either.

Patrick was looking down at her, the expression on his face a mixture of devotion and puzzlement. "A penny for your thoughts," he whispered.

But Tara shook her head. "I think that's one offer I'll turn down," she said. "After all, a girl's got to have some secrets."

Alternate cheerleader Melissa falls in love for the first time with a smooth new senior — only to discover that he's interested in Jessica, too! Read Cheerleaders #39, ALL OR NOTHING.